HOME
for
CHRISTMAS

ANDREW M. GREELEY

A TOM DOHERTY ASSOCIATES BOOK
NEW YORK

HOME FOR CHRISTMAS

Copyright © 2009 by Andrew M. Greeley Enterprises, Ltd.

Illustrations by Rhys Davies

A Forge Book
Published by Tom Doherty Associates, LLC
175 Fifth Avenue
New York, NY 10010

www.tor-forge.com

Forge® is a registered trademark of Tom Doherty Associates, LLC.

Library of Congress Cataloging-in-Publication Data

Greeley, Andrew M., 1928–
    Home for Christmas / Andrew M. Greeley.—1st hardcover ed.
      p. cm.
    "A Tom Doherty Associates book."
    ISBN 978-0-7653-2250-0
    1. Christmas stories.   I. Title.
  PS3557.R358H66 2009
  813'.54—dc22

                           2009017172

First Edition: October 2009

Printed in the United States of America

0 9 8 7 6 5 4 3 2 1

Also by Andrew M. Greeley from Tom Doherty Associates

HOME

for

CHRISTMAS

For Tatiana, whose idea it was

Eye has not seen, nor has ear heard, nor has it entered into the heart of men those things which God has prepared for those who love Him.

—ST. PAUL

NOTE

There is no reasonable doubt that near-death experiences (NDE) happen. They have been reported in India and other Asian countries as well as in the West. My colleague and friend Carol Zaleski discovered in a brilliant study incidents that fit the paradigm in the Middle Ages. Nor is there any question that usually they have a powerful impact on those who experience them. The debate is about what they mean. Atheist scholars dismiss them; believers are convinced that they have had a taste of the afterlife. Discussion between the two groups is pointless. The atheists reject such phenomena as impossible and must result from disorderly behavior of brain chemicals at the time of death. Believers, even those whose faith was never very strong, argue that they have been there and they *know*.

I approach this story from the point of view of an agnostic. I don't know what happens in such encounters with transcendence (or Transcendence). I argue that the encounters do not necessarily prove there is life after death. I do not believe that they are a solid basis for religious faith. I agree with Professor Zaleski that they are a "hint," nothing more. But nothing less either. For people who have been there, done that, there is no longer any doubt. For people like me, they are attractive hints and wonderful stories.

St. Paul tells us that we cannot imagine what the world to come is like. To which I reply, "You are right, Paul of Tarsus, as usual. But there is no law against trying to imagine—which is what I have done in this story. Moreover, we cannot help but imagine."

Such imaginations involve imagining what God is like. Therefore in this story, in the dialogue between Pete Kane and the One, I speculate about what God is like. I believe firmly and confess gladly that in this conversation I have underestimated the mercy and love of God—and also his wit. There is no way that one can comprehend the ineffable, as much as humans try. Along with St. Therese, however, I believe that God is nothing but mercy and love and the more we reflect on that, the better off we will be.

All my stories are about God. In this one, I give God a chance to speak for himself. I apologize for the inadequacies of my imagination. I insist, however, that any God worth believing in is far better than the one in my portrait.

Written with hope as I approach the beginning of the ninth decade of my life.

–Andrew Greeley
February 5, 2008

PS: The people and the places in this story are all fictional. The setting is vaguely Chicago and is influenced by many Chicago neighborhoods, but represents neither the social structure nor the population of any specific neighborhood. I do not even admit that St. Reg's has a specific location in the West Side or the North Side or the South Side. Those who see themselves in some of the characters of my story should be so lucky.

I

scene: A dusty ruined street in an Iraqi city. A cautious American patrol, perhaps two squads, probes its way through the rubble.

woman's voice: "The war here is usually quiet, yet violence and death can erupt any minute and blot out human life." Then the silence returns, save for the wail of ambulance sirens. WTN is embedded with a combat patrol of the First Cavalry Division.

Wendy Eastland, a sophisticated, self-possessed woman, appears on the monitor. Her skin is dark, her teeth flawlessly white, her accent plummy English—perhaps from South Asia with a first-rate British education. She is wearing an American fatigue uniform, armor protection, and the required steel helmet.

"The men who walk on these dangerous patrols

are only doing what is their duty. They are all brave. Rarely is the television camera in a position to capture heroism above and beyond the call of duty. Today in the space of a few seconds our camera captured two such acts of supreme bravery."

The camera returns to the street. Someone is firing at the patrol.

"Take cover!" an officer yells.

The men scatter to doorways or drop to the ground to become smaller targets. Someone throws a grenade in their midst. The officer dashes to the grenade, picks it up like a shortstop fielding a ground ball and with a fluid motion throws it across the street into the house from which the gunfire is coming. There is an explosion and smoke pours out of the house, then another deafening explosion rocks the camera. The American officer is knocked off his feet. He falls to the ground and fires at the house.

Then two tiny children, three- and two-years old perhaps, emerge out of the dust and appear on the monitor.

"Cease fire!" the officer yells as he leaps to his feet. He collects the two kids in his arms and rushes into one of the ruins on his side of the street. He is hit by a bullet, winces and grabs a weapon from one of his men.

"Resume firing!" he orders. "Give them all we got!"

He lifts his automatic weapon painfully and empties its ordnance into the house, which now crumbles into dust.

Reporter on monitor.

"This scene of war in Iraq requires more time to describe than to watch. It is a commonplace. One has to watch the replay to comprehend that the young American has saved the lives of many, perhaps most of his men and of two Iraqi toddlers."

Camera shifts back to the street. A young couple approaches the Americans hesitantly.

"Cease fire," the officer orders.

His men nervously keep their weapons aimed at the street.

The young Iraqis babble disconsolately. They want their kids. The camera zooms in on the American, the sleeve of his armor red with blood. He hands the smaller child, cradled in his good arm, to her mother and then leads the little boy out and gives him to his father. Both parents sob.

"Come on, men!" he orders them. "Let's secure this place. Follow me. Be careful—it may be booby-trapped."

He leads the patrol across the street.

"Talking to one of the members of the patrol, we learned that their commanding officer was Second Lieutenant Peter Patrick Kane from Poplar Grove, a suburb of Chicago."

Wendy is seen talking to a teenage American boy. One of the soldiers.

"Yeah, that's Pete Kane. He's something else. We're lucky to have him with us."

"Would you call him a hero?"

"Hell, yes! What else can you call him?"

"Bravery is as common among Americans here as are ambushes, gunfire, and explosions. Split-second heroism may be less common. Perhaps we captured this scene on our camera only by chance. This is Wendy Eastland, WTN, with the First Cavalry Division somewhere in Iraq."

2

TV monitor reveals an American compound.

ANCHOR: Our Wendy Eastland witnessed an extraordinary act of heroism by an American soldier in Iraq, which we reported yesterday. Now she has obtained permission to interview him.

Camera discloses Ms. Eastland, devoid of helmet and armor, sitting on a bench in front of an adobelike building. Next to her on the bench is a tall broad-shouldered American officer with close-cut, dark red hair, clad in impeccably pressed fatigues. His helmet and weapon are propped up on the wall, ready for instant use. He is every inch a promising junior officer, courteous, restrained, unemotional. He does not want to do the interview and his answers are terse. However, occasionally, his military mask slips and a

dangerous grin slips across his face. His left shoulder
is in a sling.

EASTLAND (EXTENDS THE MIKE TOWARD HIM): Thank
you for agreeing to the interview, Lt. Kane.

KANE: My CO ordered me to speak to you. You should
thank him.

EASTLAND (NOT USED TO BEING REBUFFED BY A YOUNG
MAN): Have you seen the tape we made of the fire-
fight yesterday?

KANE: No, ma'am.

EASTLAND: Might I ask why not?

KANE: The CO debriefed us last night after he had
watched the tape. He approved of our unit's behavior.

EASTLAND: Were you frightened during the incident?

KANE: No, ma'am. I was too scared to be frightened.
    Eastland glances up. She understands that she has a
difficult interviewee. This young man is not a redneck
from the hill country. Probably a troublemaking Mick.

EASTLAND: Were you afraid you might die?

KANE: Every time we go out on the streets that's a possibility, ma'am—for all of us.

EASTLAND (CHANGING HER TACK): Our cameraman said you fielded that grenade like it was a double-play grounder. Did you play baseball, Lt. Kane?

KANE: A little bit, ma'am. High school. I didn't have a major league career ahead of me.

EASTLAND: You're from . . . Poplar Grove, Illinois, Lt. Kane . . . ?

KANE: Affirmative that, ma'am.

EASTLAND: Do you have a wife or a family there?

KANE: No, ma'am.

EASTLAND: A sweetheart?

KANE: No, ma'am.

EASTLAND: No one would miss you if you die?

KANE: It's hell here for those who do. But that's what happens if you're going to fight a war with National Guard and reservists.

EASTLAND (GIVING UP): Would the folks back in Poplar Grove be surprised by your leadership out here?

KANE: They wouldn't believe it.

EASTLAND: But your troops seem to have complete faith in you?

KANE: You put a uniform and a gold bar on a kid right out of college and give him a command, he's a leader whether he wants to be or not. Incidentally, there are women in my outfit too.

A glint in his eyes as he trips her up.

EASTLAND (TRYING TO RECOVER): Do you worry about risking their lives by your orders?

KANE: I worry about risking the lives of all the soldiers under my command. I am sworn to protect their lives and the lives of innocent civilians. That's all I did yesterday.

EASTLAND: Do you think you'll survive out here?

KANE: I don't know, ma'am. Second lieutenants don't have a lot of longevity in any war. You might say a prayer for me.

Eastland turns away from the camera, which focuses in on her and forgets about Kane.

EASTLAND: Second Lt. Peter Patrick Kane doesn't look
     or talk like he's a warrior, much less a hero. Yet watch
     as we play this tape and see what you think . . . I know
     I'll say a prayer for him. I hope my viewers back home
     will do the same thing. This is Wendy Eastland with
     the First Cavalry Division outside of Baghdad.

"Peter Kane is coming home for Christmas," the young woman said.

"The return of Killer Kane."

Never was a nickname based on a comparison of opposites in such contrast to the person so dubbed. His generation had no memory of Buck Rogers and his nemesis. My own generation was not unfamiliar with it. The generation of my first pastor at least knew the implication of the words, though I cannot imagine that man reading the comic pages.

"That's a cruel nickname, Monsignor," Mariana said. "You shouldn't use it."

"I never called him that. Are we to expect a renewal of the old romance?"

Mariana was a tall, lithe young woman with long, burnished blond hair, flawless complexion, unforgiving blue eyes, the body of a model—disciplined by habitual training for the marathon—and an IQ around 175. She wore a light gray business suit, every inch the brilliant young lawyer. Not one to mess around with, monsignor or not.

"There never was a romance, Monsignor."

"What would you call the relationship which began in first grade and, unless I misunderstand the purpose of this visit to the rectory, has never ended?"

Her eyes turned to finely tempered steel.

"I hate that woman."

"The one who made him famous?"

"I don't want to go through it all over again."

"You may have to, Signorina Pellegrino."

Dead silence.

"I thought you were on the edge of engagement. With the brilliant young doctor . . ."

"Wainwright Burke. My mother thinks so."

4

In my first term at St. Regis, first assignment after ordination, I encountered Petey Pat Kane and Mariana Pia Pellegrino in my first catechetical assignment—second graders in training for their First Communion. The pastor warned me that Sister Superior would monitor me and if I was unsatisfactory she would dismiss me. He was a man who illustrated the truth that a curate was a mouse in training to be a rat and the deeper truth that a liberal curate was a rat in training to be a dragon.

Sister—who like everyone else in the parish, besides the monsignor, seemed to think I was OK—warned me beforehand that they were a good bunch of kids, except for Petey Pat Kane and Mariana Pia Pellegrino, who would take over the class unless I stopped them.

"I'll point them out to you," she promised me as we entered the classroom.

I glanced around and saw the offenders immediately.

"The blond and the redhead," I whispered.

"Right on!"

"I'm not much older than either of them."

"Good morning, boys and girls."

"Good morning, Fr. Joyce."

They were apparently upset that I had stolen their opening line.

Peter Patrick Kane was a scrawny little redhead with a quizzical—and thoroughly artificial—squint. His green eyes were alive with what my great aunt would have called divilment. Mariana Pia Pellegrino was a blond beauty, doubtless spoiled by her indulgent parents.

"I've told the boys and girls you will try to answer any of their questions."

"I'm not very smart, Sister. I won't be able to answer most of their questions, which will be too hard for me."

Mariana Pia's hand shot up—a demand for immediate response. I ignored her and called on Jane Quinlan, a name I picked off S'ter's charts.

She had a problem with what her grandmother had said about sacrilege. I pointed out that the Church had changed its discipline about the pre-Eucharist fast. After I had ignored her four times, Mariana Pia gave up. She didn't sulk, however.

The little redhead raised his hand. His green eyes were twinkling with mischief.

"Reverend Father, Mariana Pia wanted to ask you a question. She always wants to ask a question. She's awfully smart."

Everyone laughed, including the blushing towhead. Even S'ter laughed.

"Mariana Pia . . ."

"She's this one, Reverend Father." He pointed at the girl in the desk next to him. "She's the blond one—natural blond, she says!"

More laughter.

"Petey Pat is my agent, Father. He's very bold. S'ter says he's a bold stump."

"Your question, Mariana Pia?" I said, trying to be stern.

It worked. Class calmed down.

"Father, how small does the bread have to be before Jesus isn't there anymore?"

Her mother had suggested that one had to be very careful not to step on a speck of Jesus as she walked away from the altar.

The mother was a scrup and so was the daughter. She articulated a perfectly reasonable theory that alleged that even a speck of a host that you could see only in a microscope might still be Jesus. She even quoted from the Pange Lingua, the Holy Thursday hymn.

"Gosh," Petey Pat observed, "if Jesus was worried about that, he should have become a jelly bean."

Another surge of laughter.

"I'm the teacher, Petey Pat. I get the laughs. Anymore wise remarks from you and you're out of the room."

The charmingly obnoxious little redhead shrunk into his desk so he was almost invisible. The class froze. Good—they were afraid of me. Mariana Pia rose to the defense of her tormentor.

"He didn't mean to make trouble, Father. Petey Pat is really very shy."

I'd better be careful, I thought. I wouldn't want to make his fierce little Amazon an enemy.

"Jesus did not want us to become obsessive about such things, Mariana Pia. In the early days of the Church, sailors would put Holy Communion on the masts of their ships, and soldiers put them on their battle flags because they knew he wanted to be near us all the time."

"Thank you, Father."

"You're welcome."

"Interesting pair," I said to S'ter as we left the room.

"They're in love with each other. Both of them very smart and very vulnerable. Difficult family backgrounds. I am afraid for them."

"Young love."

"I've seen it before. Young but very intense."

I worried about them as I returned to the rectory. Very attractive children. What would happen to them?

I settled into my tattered easy chair to wait for the monsignor. He came to my room almost immediately, holding a travel magazine in his hand. I was sure he had phoned S'ter as soon as he had heard me trudging up the stairs.

"Well, Sr. Joan Marie said you didn't make too much of a fool out of yourself."

In my first years at St. Regis he never once paid me a compliment. He complimented no one.

"That was good of her."

"So I suppose we'll have to let you continue for a while in your instructions."

"OK."

"Any specially bright children?"

"Peter Kane."

"I wouldn't waste my time on him, if I were you. His parents are immigrants—father a truck driver, wife a whimpering bitch. Nothing there."

The pastor had been a snob all his life. He grew up Back of the Yards, marched in the Industrial Areas Foundation protests and became one of the last "labor priests" in the diocese. Yet the day he was appointed to St. Regis, he acted like he had been installed on the Queen's annual Honors List. The joke in the parish behind his back was that you had to submit your last three federal tax returns before you could become one of his cronies.

"Anyone else?"

"Mariana Pellegrino."

"Mariana *Pia*!"

"Yeah."

"Her family is very important. The father is Don Silvio Pellegrino, managing partner of the largest law firm on LaSalle Street and the last American ambassador to the Vatican. Powerful contacts over there. Major contributor to the parish. High-class gentleman."

"Sil" was, in my judgment, a pompous ass from the Italian neighborhood around Taylor Street who had made his early money by defending Outfit thugs.

"And her mother is a Carter—Dr. Wellington Carter's daughter."

He intended that I be impressed. I was not.

"She is active in Catholic charities. Quite close to the cardinal."

Anita Carter Pellegrino, as she called herself, was an anorexic bitch whom even other affluent matrons of the parish couldn't stand. Both she and Sil had grown up in Bridgeport and had, it was alleged, waited for their first million-dollar year to announce their conversion—to the Republican party.

I offered no comment. In the pastor's world view I was shanty

Irish, though he knew full well that my family could buy and sell all his cronies in the parish.

He stormed back into my cell a half hour later.

"Anita Carter Pellegrino just called me. Didn't I tell you that they were important people?"

"I had the impression that you thought so, yes."

"You are a fool, Father. An immature arrogant fool."

"That might be the case," I admitted.

"She tells me that you were encouraging sacrilege in the First Communion instructions today."

"Really?"

"She said that you told those innocent children that the early Christians affixed the Eucharist to their battle flags and the masts of their ships."

"That's true, Monsignor," I said reaching for my source. "It's right there in—"

"Like all overeducated young people, Father, you think wisdom comes from books. You do not have the simple elementary common sense to protect little children from such blasphemous and sacrilegious notions. I am hereby dismissing you from all catechetical work in this parish and specifically ordering you to stay out of the second-grade classrooms."

"Suit yourself," I said indifferently.

But I was not indifferent. I liked the second graders. We had established common grounds that afternoon. It didn't matter, however—I would be out of here soon enough.

I almost asked him if he was going to preach at my Sunday masses. That would scare the living daylights out of him. He said the 6:30 A.M. and didn't preach.

As I walked to the basketball courts when school was getting out a week later, I encountered Peter and Mariana, both looking very disconsolate.

"S'ter says you won't teach our class anymore," Peter said sadly.

"It's not fair," Mariana said.

"And it's our fault," Peter concluded.

"Peter! It is not! It's my bitch of a mother's fault!"

"Don't talk that way, Mariana. You shouldn't call your mother that."

"My father calls her that all the time."

So, trouble in paradise.

"S'ter says we could talk to you out on the courts after school."

"She says Monsignor never looks at the courts, because he doesn't like teens."

"Especially girl teens."

"Very bad taste on his part," I said.

"Would you ever just talk to us?" Irish polite subjunctive.

"I would!"

"See you tomorrow. Some of the other kids will come too."

So for the rest of their First Communion year Mariana and Petey and Jane Quinlan and Marty Finn and Collette Worski and Joe Charles and Tommy O'Brien and Reen Connors and I talked about God and Church and heaven and hell every day that it didn't rain or snow. I don't know how much they learned, but I learned a lot. For of such are the kingdom.

Petey Kane was the precinct captain in charge. He decided when we would meet, who was legitimately excused, whose turn it was to ask a question, who was not satisfied with an answer, when it was time to break up and go home. He and Mariana Pia (whom he often called Mary Anne the Pious) were foils one for another, reveling in the give-and-take of their arguments.

"Sometimes you are just too smart," he protested, "for your own good."

"Well, I'll let you have some of it because you are not smart enough," she said, her face turning crimson—its color half the time. The rest of the bunch laughed on cue. We all had learned just how fragile Mariana was and how she depended on Petey for reassurance.

"Most men don't like smart women," Petey continued. "I am an exception."

The girls laughed in derision.

"I like all of you," he said innocently. "Let's get on with our discussion of angels—right, Reverend Father?"

"He just wants to hide behind you, Father!" Mariana protested.

"Is that a nice thing for an angel to say!"

Groans from the class.

One afternoon Petey wasn't there.

"He's got a black eye," Joe Charles said.

"No disgrace in that."

After we broke up that session—none of them lasted more than fifteen minutes—Mariana remained with me while the others left.

"Pete's father beats him up all the time," she said, averting her eyes from mine. "Just for the fun of it. Please don't tell him I told you, Father."

Then she turned and, with tears running down her cheeks, ran away from me. I would later learn that Patrick Kane routinely beat all his children, and on occasion his wife. Jane Quinlan cornered me later that week and filled me in on the mothers. Mrs. Kane thought that Petey had no business hanging around the daughter of such an important family. Mrs. Pellegrino thought that the Kanes were trash and forbade her daughter to have anything to do with Petey Pat. Mariana simply ignored her.

These kids were my first children and would always have a special place in my heart. I worried about them often through the years, Peter Kane especially. The little redhead was too sensitive for one his age. Even quick-witted leprechauns have feelings, even if they were skilled community organizers. He would not have Mariana around all his life, to envelop him in her magic smile when he had made a mistake. He pretended that he was protecting her, but it was evident to me that at some point during second grade, the roles had changed. The other kids (and I was one of them for our magic minutes together) hadn't figured that out.

For second graders, these kids were learning a lot about social class.

That summer S'ter Joan Marie was dismissed from her twin role as superior and second grade teacher. She had run afoul of Monsignor once too often. Her order "punished" her by making her president of their college in central Iowa. I lasted my appointed six years at the parish and then was removed at the monsignor's insistence just before the big financial scandal broke. Monsignor went into honorary retirement. The rumor spread throughout the parish that I had been replaced because the scandal was my fault. However, the state's attorney's office cleared me completely and the cardinal assigned me to graduate work in liturgical theology at Sant' Anselmo

University in Rome, even writing me a letter praising my integrity and probity during the crisis.

Nonetheless I slipped out of the parish one step ahead of the vigilantes—the monsignor's cronies. Not a very dignified exit. My onetime First Communicants met me in the rectory office and promised that they would never forget our years together. They had all changed, the girls becoming young women almost overnight in the summer after fifth grade, poised and self-possessed in their new roles as they had been as little girls. Puberty for the boys was more difficult the following year. Petey Pat was no longer the laughing little leprechaun. He was now a sullen runt of whom his classmates made fun. He was clumsy in deed and word and too smart for his own good. He knew the answers to everything and was damned as a walking eynclopedia.

His tormentors left him alone when Mariana was present.

"Petey has geeked out," she explained to me. "But he won't always be a geek, will he, Father?"

"Geekiness is not inevitable," I said cautiously.

"I pray for him every night," she said. "He's so good and so sweet when the real geeks are not around."

"We'll just have to give him time."

"He'll be fine," she said with stubborn confidence.

Neither of us could have guessed what would happen to Petey Pat Kane.

5

ANCHOR: WTN has learned that the three troopers of the First Cavalry Division, held hostage by Sunni terrorists, have been freed just as the insurgents were preparing to decapitate Specialist First Class Irene Rayburn. Wendy Eastland of our Baghdad Bureau reports.

EASTLAND: A commando force from the cavalry, under the command of now Capt. Peter Patrick "Killer" Kane, broke into the terrorist safe house, immobilized them with flash-bang grenades, freed the prisoners, and eliminated the terrorist cell. Only one trooper was wounded by a blow from the sword that had been aimed at Specialist Rayburn's neck. Maj. Gen. Fred Rogers provided a few more details.

The footage switches to Gen. Rogers, a trim, incisive West Pointer with flawlessly pressed fatigues and reading glasses. He seems shaken by the story he tells.

ROGERS: At fifteen thirty this afternoon Capt. Kane reported that he had a tip as to the location of the house in which our troopers were being held. His information indicated that one of them was to be executed on television this evening after dark. He asked permission to attempt a raid on the house; I immediately approved the plan. His team surrounded the house without alerting the enemy to their presence. They used smoke and stun bombs to gain entrance and engaged in a brief fight with the terrorists. One of them was holding a large ceremonial sword over Specialist Rayburn's head. He was immediately eliminated. The terrorists were would-be suicide bombers who used the house as storage for their explosives. They attempted to ignite the explosives, but our troopers prevented that. The casualties were six terrorists dead and one of ours wounded by a sword. The prisoners are now free and unharmed. The wounded trooper's current status, I am told, is serious but not critical.

EASTLAND: Capt. Kane?

ROGERS (HESITATES): I can't say anything about casualties until next of kin are notified.

EASTLAND: You have the TV camera. Did it record any of the encounter?

ROGERS: All of the encounter. It is very brief.

EASTLAND: You will make it available to the media?

ROGERS: That decision will be made at higher levels. We will have to consider the threats to the security of our troops if the enemy knows what they look like.

EASTLAND: Was it hand-to-hand combat?

ROGERS: I think you may assume that it was, in such close quarters. We did not want to kill any of our own with stray bullets.

EASTLAND: Was the decision made to kill all the enemy before the attack?

ROGERS: I believe that our men knew that the house was filled with explosives. I can assure you there was no deliberate killing.

EASTLAND (SPEAKING TO ANCHOR): That's all we can learn here, Cynthia. A complete news blackout has been imposed on the First Cav. No one is talking. Yet the hostages are free and the terrorists are dead, with only one American casualty.

CYNTHIA: Capt. Kane?

EASTLAND: Presumably.

CYNTHIA: Will you try to interview him?

EASTLAND: I don't think he likes journalists, but this is one of them, Wendy Eastland, World Television News, Baghdad.

6

Eastland and Kane in a quiet corner of a hospital tent. Kane, in hospital gown smeared with blood, looks terrible, haggard, tired, sedated. He is trussed up in a bed with monitors and medical bottles hooked up to both arms. The wild look in his eyes suggests that his daemon has been unleashed.

KANE: You always see me, Ms. Eastland, at something less than my best.

EASTLAND: I told Gen. Rogers I did not want to force you into the interview.

KANE: He knew there was no way he could force me to talk about it.

EASTLAND: How long did the encounter take?

KANE: They tell me it covered seventy-three seconds on the tape.

EASTLAND: You had rehearsed your roles before forcing your way into the house?

KANE: Certainly. It was a quick and rough rehearsal. Apparently it was enough . . .

EASTLAND: Will you advocate the release of the tape?

KANE: No. It isn't exciting, Ms. Eastland; your viewers would find it boring. Hand-to-hand fighting in a smoke-filled room. Cries, orders, curses, prayers—not at all like a film. Boring. Death is almost always boring.

EASTLAND: Will you be sent home?

KANE: Why would they send me home, Ms. Eastland? I've just been redeployed over here. I'll be as good as new in a couple of days. Incidentally, Wendy, you promised that you would pray for me, last time we talked . . .

EASTLAND: I did.

KANE: Keep it up!

EASTLAND: I will.

7

"That was our Petey Pat, Mariana."

"He was showing off, Father, for that gorgeous woman, like he always showed off for me before he went geeky."

"He had a terrible adolescence. It is very hard to grow into a man when you have such parents."

"His mom is all right. She tells me what he says in his e-mails to her. She thinks I have a right to know what's happening. Besides, the father has calmed down since Petey knocked him out."

"Our Petey knocked his father out?"

"When we had the prom accident, Mr. Kane went after him with his black thorn stick. Petey took the stick away from him and put him out . . . with one punch."

"Petey Pat Kane!"

"No one had noticed how big and strong he had become because he was still into geekiness. He told his father if he ever hit anyone in the family again he'd come back and kill him. I don't think he meant it, but he sure scared Mr. Kane. Everyone knew about it."

"I was enjoying spring in Rome."

"You didn't miss much, Father."

"I heard that you were pretty impressive yourself."

"I suppose that bitch Janie Quinlan sent you the tape of my performance in front of St. Reg's?"

"And she told me how you and your father forced the cops to clear Petey. I must say, Mariana, you looked good in mourning."

She sniffed.

"He didn't even say thank you or good-bye. He just went home to beat up his father and then left for school and the army. I've never seen him again. He's still a geek. When he is deployed home, he takes classes at that geeky Texas A&M place."

"Studying for a master's in military history."

"Do you see him much, Father?"

"Twice. He usually stays away from Poplar Grove."

"Does he ask about me, Father?"

"Get real, Mariana! Of course he does!"

"And what do you say?"

"I say the two of you still have an agenda."

"He's in love with that TV witch."

"She is happily married to an important American diplomat."

"Whatever."

8

I should have written before now, Mariana. In fact I tried a number of times. Never knew what to say. I want to apologize for being a geek for so many years. We had a little action here today and WTN reported on it, like they did after our last little dustup. I want to tell you not to worry about me. I'll be home alive and well someday soon and then maybe we can have a long talk.

Or even a short talk.

Love,

Pete

He paused over the document and then deleted it.

9

"You feeling any better, soldier?"

"No, General, but it's nice of you to ask."

"That was a very good interview yesterday with your friend Wendy."

"The meds made me more charming than I usually am."

"Or unleashed your Irish blarney. Turns out that when you're wearing that mask you are very good at it."

"Which makes me dangerous, huh?"

"I looked up your record. You spend your time at Fort Hood in school."

"Keeps me out of trouble, sir."

"A master's degree in military history?"

"I hope to finish the next time at Fort Hood."

"And then?"

"Then I'll be redeployed back here."

"Perhaps a doctorate?"

"Maybe."

He frowned.

"The army needs its intellectual officers, men who think about what we do and criticize. Prevents future mistakes."

"All we can reasonably ask of them is that they help us to understand past mistakes."

"Sometimes they aren't able to do even that, though it's not for want of effort."

"Civilian leadership," Pete murmured.

"Our intellectuals are supposed to give us the arguments to guide the civilian leaders. That's the tension they are caught in."

He was saying more than a general ought to be saying to a newly minted captain. What was he up to?

"I have reason to believe, soldier, that I am going to rise pretty far in this man's army. I'm not sure I want to do that. But I won't turn it down either. If you ever need help, let me know. And even if you don't, let me know. I'll be in the background."

"Thank you, sir."

There were too many sedatives running around in Pete's body for him to fully understand what Rogers was saying.

"Most men in my position would have rejected your request to conduct a raid."

"Yes, sir."

"You would have done it anyhow?"

"Yes, sir."

"I figured as much."

He smiled broadly.

"Go to sleep, son. We'll talk again some day."

He was recruiting the new captain for something. Pete didn't like that.

But he was intrigued.

With my dissertation almost finished from the Anselmianum I took a month off to return to my archdiocese to discover whether I was still in good paper with my cardinal. It turned out that I was, despite some negative feedback from my former pastor's cronies about the monsignor's conviction for embezzlement—along with that of the parish's financial director. These cronies insisted that the monsignor was innocent and that I had masterminded the whole deal.

"As though you needed the money," the cardinal said.

"The monsignor could never accept the fact that my family had more money than any of his cronies."

"So I gathered."

I told him about my dissertation.

"I assumed that you would come up with something that would cause a lot of trouble. Congratulations."

The cardinal was not a bomb thrower exactly. But he liked to have a few of them around.

"Are you going out to St. Regis?"

"Incommunicado, as some of your friends in the Curia might say. One troubled teen to check up on."

"Your former pastor said that you cared only about the kids and not about the important people."

"Guilty as charged. But you don't make any money on kids."

"Not in the short run, James."

"There's that."

I didn't bother to tell him that I had some offers for more or less permanent employment in the Vatican. I was sick of Rome, a dirty and disorderly place, and of the Roman Curia where I could easily have lost my soul.

So I was sitting in the Ice Cream Factory, an emporium across from the railroad station crowded with soda fountain memorabilia and the best ice cream in the state of Illinois—a mom-and-pop shop run by a grim and sour middle-aged couple, both of whom hated kids.

"What are you doing back here?" the woman of the house demanded when I joined Peter Kane at one of the art deco tables. "I thought they got rid of you."

"I came back to cause more trouble," I said. "Mr. Kane and I will start with two chocolate malts with a double order of whipped cream and don't try to cheat us."

I had discovered when I was an associate pastor in Forest Grove that these people were only happy when they encountered someone they could really dislike—such as a malted-milk-swirling teenage priest.

"Still trying out for the Cubs?" I asked and pointed at his shortstop's mitt.

"I'm never going to be that good, Fr. Jimmy."

Outside the ancient trees of Poplar Park were dressing for autumn against a disapproving gray sky. Pete Kane's mood seemed to fit the setting. He was still a string bean, a tall, clumsy, self-conscious kid who did look geeky. He was still going through the transformation that some young men experience in their freshman year of high school—his lean and hungry body filling out with the solid muscles of young adulthood and his bloodstream boiling with the hormones that mark this advent of adulthood. Unfortunately, those hormones do not provide either the wisdom or the under-standing of what this new male body is capable of, save for scooping up a ground ball and rifling it at the first baseman.

"I heard that you led the team in batting and you went to the district finals. Not bad for the first year in the league."

"I didn't play much," he said, sinking into a sad-sack slouch that must have been his favorite posture for the last couple of years.

"Why not?"

"Neil Elgin wanted to play shortstop. Most of the guys said he was better." He shrugged his shoulders. "Maybe he was."

My elfin little redhead had morphed into a creep.

"Then," he added, "my father started coming to the games. He told everyone what they were doing wrong. Lot of curse words. He came out on the field and knocked me down when I missed a line drive. The coach asked him never to come back. We lost the game and Neil started the next game and played for the rest of the season. Turned out he wasn't very good. But the guys had stopped liking me long before that. I knew I was in trouble when they stopped laughing at my jokes and made fun of me in the classroom."

A leprechaun should never change into a sad sack, but what could he do if his father was a disgrace?

"You're playing at St. Bellarmine in the spring?"

"I don't think so. They absorbed our whole team. Our coach is a cop. Neil's father is a cop. That's that."

"Our old First Communion crowd?"

"They've all changed, Father. The boys are all girl crazy and the girls are all boy crazy."

"Hormones, Pete."

"I understand that, Father. However you make a fool out of yourself, it's even worse."

He slouched even deeper into his chair and scarcely managed to drink his malt. With a moron as a father how would he get through the years ahead?

"Mariana?" I asked tentatively.

"She's the most stuck-up of them all."

"Not the frightened little stranger who showed up back in second grade?"

"She doesn't need an agent anymore, Father."

"Maybe a knight on a white horse."

"I'm not applying for the job."

"Still playing ball, though?"

"For the American Legion team—the league that picks up superannuated Little League players."

"Big word."

"Gets me in trouble. Mariana tells me I'm showing off. The guys in the class make fun of me. I tell her that she's the biggest showoff in Poplar Grove."

"And she gets angry and cries."

"That's what they all do. I am fed up with women."

Maybe maturity and intelligence and thirty more pounds of muscle would see him through this terrible time. But with his father around?

"So what's next?"

"If I play well enough, I might get a scholarship to college. If not, I'll go to State College and get a military scholarship—ROTC or something like that. I just have to get out of this place and forget it. I'll never come back, never again."

I prayed for him on the train back to Chicago. I thought about calling Mariana. That would, I told myself, not be a very good idea.

A lot of stars tonight. Baghdad, for a change, was quiet. I couldn't sleep. My side was still sore from that Islamic sword. The swordsman still comes after me in my dreams, poor crazy man. He has just cut off Mariana's head and I plunge my bayonet into his stomach, just as his sword cuts into me. It's all mixed up in my dreams. He was trying to kill Specialist Rayburn, not Mariana, and I kill him before he decapitates his victim. Like the others he was high on dope. We surprised and frightened them. They never had a chance. But they still wanted to kill us.

When Mariana invades my dreams, they become erotic. All my old fantasies rushing back from the past, an avalanche of lust. Or maybe of love. With the Mariana of my dreams, it's hard to tell.

The stars in the Iraqi sky remind me of the stars over Poplar Grove on the night that Collette and Joey were killed. It was all my fault. If I hadn't walked down to the river with Mariana to make out, they both would still be alive.

We had kissed each other often when we were little kids and then when we reached a certain age—nine or ten—we just stopped. There was something more at work than childish affection. We didn't understand it and were scared. We avoided each other, Mariana more subtly than I, so it always looked like I was the geek, which God knows I was. During our years in high school we hardly said a word to each other. But I was obsessed with her body. Awake and asleep I wanted her, I was hungry for her. I imagined taking her by force. I would never have done that, of course. We had told each other as kids that we would marry some day and that till then we were engaged. We had no idea exactly what marriage involved and when I understood what it was about I was horrified and hungry at the same time. I wondered whether she felt the same way I did. The contempt of teenage boys for women is the result of fear. You must dominate them or . . . or they will humiliate you.

Then she invited me to the prom. I hated proms, without ever knowing what young people did at them. At Bellarmine high school they usually made out and tested how far they could go with one another. I almost turned her down. Then I realized that I could make out with her and maybe find out how far I could go. She wouldn't have any choice. So I accepted her invitation after some show of reluctance and contempt for her and for the whole idea of proms. That Joey and Collette would be with us did not matter. She asked me if I would drive her car because, as she said, everyone in Bellarmine knew that I did not drink. During the next week my blood must have been dense with hormones. Yet the young woman for whom I had bought a corsage and rented a tuxedo was also my old friend. It would be good to talk to her again. Nothing made sense anymore. Did one engage in sexual experimentation (a phrase

I did not use or even know at the time) with someone who is an old friend?

Mr. Pellegrino opened the door for me with the courtesy of one Italian noble welcoming another. I had certainly grown up in a hurry, hadn't I? But that's what young people do to their parents, isn't it? Fine work on the baseball team. Too bad that the schools don't put more emphasis on scholarships. Any scholarship offers? St. Ben's? Good place, hope you get it. Mariana tells me you're going to drive the car because everyone knows you don't drink. No violations, I noticed. We Italians don't believe you can have a good party without some red wine around.

Then Mariana came down the stairs, a radiant golden marchesa prepared for a royal ball. A woman who was chaste and sexy in the same instant. We advanced a step toward each other and stopped. Breathless. You are so beautiful, Mariana, I said, stumbling like the geek I still was. You certainly do justice to that tuxedo, Petey Pat. I'll take good care of her, sir. I know you will, son. Standard lines that meant I would get her home alive, sober, and unpregnant.

We began chattering as we walked down the front stairs of the ornate Victorian house on the top of the hill from which the Pellegrinos looked down at the rest of the neighborhood, catching up on all the news and gossip since grade school. Mariana and Pete together again as they always had been. Whatever had changed between us now went away. She flipped the keys to her own personal Jaguar to me. My fate is in your hands, Peter Patrick. We would recall later, though separately, the irony of that comment.

We picked up Joey and Collette at the Worski house where we posed for a battery of pictures of the beautiful young foursome, two of which would not survive prom night. Jane Quinlan sent me copies of the pictures at State U later on. I tore them up, wept, and then hated myself for the terrible waste.

Much later, after my social science courses at State, I began to understand the peculiar dynamic of the senior prom. At its best it helps some young men and women cross for the first time the boundary between adolescence and adulthood, to realize that the other was really a Thou that we must treat with reverence and respect. Thus we could become friends again as we had been when we were in the school yard before First Communion.

The passionate kissing that night was a celebration that we were now free again to love one another. It should have been a turning point in our lifelong friendship. You are really good at this kissing deal, Petey Pat, she had said, taking a very deep breath, down at the side of Poplar Creek. You must be a natural because I know you haven't had much practice. At that point I knew that there was much more that I might have done. But she was Mariana and I couldn't treat her that way. I often think that if it had not been for the accident we would now be a happily married couple with two kids and an established habit of adjusting to our differences. Something new was born that night, but it died very quickly.

The clouds cover the stars now and I'm not in Poplar Grove; not in the park by the river where we exchanged our most passionate kiss and sealed the doom of our two friends.

12

The cardinal peered at me over the top of his rimless glasses.

"I would say, Jimmy, that your teachers have gauged your talents and personality quite accurately. I had no trouble recognizing the author of this dissertation." He lifted the thick book with some effort.

"I didn't try to hide, Cardinal."

"I doubt that you could if you wanted to. As your former pastor remarked to me, you don't give a shit about the Church, only about people."

"Fair enough, I suppose."

"And the good abbot on the Anselmianum says that you will make a very interesting vicar for Divine Worship—if I am not troubled by having someone in that role who is free of obsession about rubrics and rules but deeply concerned about serving the worshiping congregation."

"You didn't need him to tell you that."

"No, I suppose not. In any case, I have here a letter to you in which you are named Vicar for Divine Worship in the Archdiocese. I outline your duties and responsibilities in such a way that will enable you to proceed cautiously, I trust in the directions toward which the Spirit is moving us."

"Thank you, Cardinal, I will do my best."

"I take that for granted. . . . There is one more thing, Father. As you know, as a penalty for our previous follies we do not have enough priests. Therefore I have to insist that all our chancery office vicars must assume the pastorate of a parish. They will be named monsignors so that it is clear that they belong to my staff."

"The Vicar for Divine Worship, more than anyone else, should be a pastor. But, Cardinal, save the purple buttons."

"My mind is made up on that. Do you want to know the name of the parish?"

"That would be nice."

"It is the parish with which you are not unfamiliar: St. Francis Regis in Poplar Grove."

I was startled and delighted.

"I thought—"

"You will find it difficult, I am sure. The man with whom I replaced the previous pastor was not the right one for the task. I have been told by some of the people of the parish that you are the only person who might be able to heal the wounds. I assume from the joy on your face that you are willing to accept this delicate and difficult work?"

"When can I start?"

"Today if you wish. And you report to me and no one else in this office. Is that clear?"

"You bet," I said as I ran for the door.

13

"Like the proverbial bad penny, I always return," I told the congregation at the 10:00 A.M. Mass on Sunday. "I plan on staying."

A huge burst of applause. Tears formed in my eyes.

"Thank you. I don't deserve it. I'll try always to be honest with you."

Janie Quinlan, pregnant with her first child, was waiting for me after Mass with her new husband, Marty Finn. She was teaching second grade at our school and wanted me to promise to visit her students next year when she was teaching First Communicants.

"You guys make me feel old."

"There's another thing you gotta do, Father. You gotta get Pete and Mariana together again. That's the most important problem in the whole parish. Like totally."

"I'll do what I can. What's the problem?"

"Those deaths on prom night. The parish has never recovered.

We'll bring over the tape and show it to you. When can we come?"

"Tuesday?"

"Great, Fr. Jim."

"It is totally essential."

14

ANCHOR: There's been a tragic accident in Poplar Grove. Two seniors from St. Bellarmine School in Poplar are dead after a fatal accident at a four-way stop near Poplar Park. Our Angela Kinkaid is there.

KINKAID: It's a mess out here, Linda. The rain has been pouring for hours. There's blood mixed with the rainwater in the gutters. The police are trying to control the crowd of spectators. Dead are Joseph Charles of Park Street and Collette Worski of McLain Avenue. The cars belong to two prominent citizens of Poplar Grove, Police Capt. Lee Elgin and attorney Silvio Pellegrino, onetime American ambassador to the Vatican. Police have already charged Peter Kane, who was driving the Jaguar owned by Mr. Pellegrino, with DUI and vehicular manslaughter and have taken him to police headquarters for questioning. The other car, this Lincon SUV over here, belongs to Capt. Elgin's son, Neil. Lt. Marble, will you describe to us how the accident occurred.

MARBLE: It went down this way, ma'am. Young Neil Elgin obeyed the four-way stop sign and then began to enter the intersection. Thereupon the driver of the Jaguar behind him, a punk named Peter Kane, ignored the stop sign and drove into the intersection at a high rate of speed. He plowed into the rear of the Lincoln, spinning it around. The young couple in the backseat apparently died instantly.

A large crowd mills around the scene of the accident, some in the dark, some illuminated by the lightning. Many in the crowd are wearing prom clothes. The young women are sobbing.

KINKAID: The backseat of the Lincoln.

MARBLE: No, ma'am, you don't get it. The backseat of the Jaguar. Their bodies have just been removed to Grove Hospital.

"Fake!" I shouted. "And a clumsy one at that! The fix was in already. No way did it happen that way. The Jaguar was already in the intersection when the Navigator ran the stop sign and crushed the kids in the backseat. Furthermore, this camera on the drive-by window of the bank should have caught the whole thing. Did anyone . . . ?"

Jane Quinlan-Finn punched the stop button on the remote. "Mr. Pellegrino the next day, Father. By then it was too late." She pushed the start button.

REPORTER: Young woman, young woman! May I ask you some questions?

> The camera focuses on Mariana Pia. She seems dazed. Her blond hair hangs lankly over her face. The rain has ruined her prom dress. She is trembling. Tears and rain pour down her face.

REPORTER: Can I ask your name?

> She hesitates.

MARIANA: Mariana Pia Pellegrino.

REPORTER: The death car belongs to your father?

MARIANA: Yes.

REPORTER: Did you have his permission to drive it tonight?

MARIANA: Yes.

REPORTER: Why did you permit Mr. . . . .ah . . . Kane to drive it?

MARIANA: Because he is a good driver.

REPORTER: How much had he been drinking?

MARIANA: He doesn't drink.

REPORTER: The police have charged him with DUI.

MARIANA: The fix is in.

REPORTER: Were you or the others in your car drinking?

MARIANA: I'm a lawyer's daughter. I am perfectly willing to take a sobriety test, but the police have not asked me. The others in the car are dead. I assume there will be an autopsy.

REPORTER: Are there any bottles of liquor in your Lincoln, Ms. Pellegrino?

MARIANA: You keep getting it wrong! That's what the cops want everyone to do. My father's car is the Jaguar. The Navigator crashed into the back of the Jaguar. It's obvious that they hit us.

REPORTER (HAUGHTILY): Well, Ms. Pellegrino, we'll have to see what the police say.

Lt. Marble appears next on the screen.

MARBLE: No ma'am, the Jaguar ran into the Navigator. There's no doubt about it. The fact that Ms. Pellegrino is the daughter of a very rich man will have no bearing on the police investigation. She is obviously trying to cover for her friend.

"That cop better have good insurance. That was libel."

Marty Finn stopped the player and magnified the image on the monitor.

He pointed to a group of big guys with bottles in their hands, laughing and carrying on.

"Neil . . . He's grown a bit, hasn't he?"

"He's a big bully!"

"Football hero," Jane snapped. "He brags that the cops can't touch him."

"I'm surprised the cops didn't get them out of the picture."

"We were there by then and the cops were avoiding them, like they didn't want to notice they were hanging around."

"We collected Reen and Tom and went down to the police station to see what they might be doing to Petey. They wouldn't let us talk to him and they had not permitted him to call a lawyer. We invaded the police station and they threw us out. So we called the TV stations and told them. They came out the next morning to interview us. There we were in our prom clothes. Before we could say anything the cops arrested us on charges of disorderly conduct. They wouldn't let us talk to lawyers because we were still juveniles."

So the police chief was interviewed and he said that there was no doubt that Petey was drunk. He and his friend Mariana Pellegrino were certainly morally responsible for the deaths of their two friends and he personally would recommend to the district attorney that he pursue the strongest possible penalties against them and their parents.

Then Mrs. Charles was on the television. She sobbed and said that Pete ought to be sent to the gas chamber and Mariana to life in prison. The media was milking the scandal for all it was worth.

Mrs. Charles, an obese, confused woman, appears on the screen, making the most of her pain.

Charles: I won't be satisfied unless I see them both frying in hell for eternity!

The next actor is Fr. Theobold, the president of Bellarmine high school.

Theobold: I decided this morning that we will tolerate no more proms at Bellarmine. They are shameless exercises in self-display at best and orgies of drinking and sex at worst. If parents cannot control their children during the closing weeks of the senior year, we will take steps to eliminate events that encourage immorality.

Reporter: Father, will the accused young people be permitted to graduate from high school?

Theobold: Certainly not! I will not permit these unruly young people to besmirch the honor of Bellarmine.

"Don Silvio probably didn't like that."

"Well, the next day was the wake," Jane said. "Petey was still in jail and Mariana's parents wouldn't let her go near either of the wakes."

All the television stations had someone talking about the problems with young people. Even church schools couldn't control the sex and alcohol and drugs. The deaths of Collette and Joe were typical of a much deeper problem of the wild children of the affluent.

The president of St. Ben's got into the act. "I have instructed the athletic director to withdraw the proffered athletic scholarship to the young man who was responsible for the accident in which two of his friends were killed. We do not need that kind of man in our campus community."

"Such good Christians, all of these people," I said.

Jane pushed the remote again.

The setting was outside St. Regis church, delicate gothic spires surrounded by delicate new leaves of a late spring under an approving blue sky. Two black hearses pulled up in front of the entrance and two copper-colored coffins were carried solemnly into the church by their classmates while the bells tolled the grief of the community. A procession of clergy paraded solemnly down the main aisle of the church to welcome these two fine young people—from my First Communion class. The abbot from St. Ben's, as well as Fr. Theobold and the old monsignor were among them.

This had happened six years ago, but for Jane, Marty, and myself it had happened only yesterday. If I had been here . . . I wouldn't have done anything because there was nothing to do. Then as the Eucharist began, a solitary figure in a long black dress and veil walked around the perimeter of the church, rosary in hand.

"Mariana," Jane whispered.

"Who else?"

"She even looks good in mourning, doesn't she?"

The camera focused on her as she stopped in front of the church. A reporter approached her.

"May I ask you a few questions, Ms. Pellegrino?"

Mariana nodded gracefully.

"Do you have any comment on Mrs. Charles's call for the death penalty?"

"Mrs. Charles has suffered a terrible loss. Her heart is broken. I can't blame her for her pain."

"Do you think there should be death penalties in these cases of driving under the influence?"

Mariana launched her carefully prepared legal brief.

"I agree with the Pope that there shouldn't be death penalties for anything. However, one of the terrible falsehoods you people have spread is that Peter was drunk. Everyone in the school knew that he didn't drink. Most thought he was weird. You might ask the police why they haven't released the results of Peter's blood test. They haven't because they know it would clear him. Instead they keep him locked up in jail and beat him because he won't confess, even though they have strong evidence that he is innocent. You might want to report on that phenomenon too. Also, you should reexamine your tapes and observe Neil Elgin and his cronies, waving whiskey bottles and drinking while the bodies were being removed. You might want to ask the police why they didn't take action and why they searched my father's car looking for bottles, but did not search Neil's car. You might wonder why they describe a collision that was quite impossible and ignore the one that actually happened and is recorded on instruments to which they have access, and on the skid marks that are still there this morning. You might ask the students from St. Reg's, weeping in the church over friends they will miss for the rest of their lives, if Neil did not often brag that the police would never dare touch him because he was the captain's son. You might start asking all those questions before someone else does and you look like the blind fools you really are."

"Are you charging a police cover-up, Ms. Pellegrino?"

"And a cover-up by the whole community and the whole county and you and your colleagues, for which we who loved Collette and Joey will never forgive you as long as you live. You are even worse than Neil Elgin and his thugs. May God have mercy on your souls."

She turned on her high heel and walked away from the camera.

"Oh boy!" I exclaimed.

"And at that very moment the cops were releasing Pete from the police station and Brother Elvin from Bellarmine was driving him home. His father came after him with a club, as his sister Ellen told us later. Peter knocked him out—twice—packed his clothes, grabbed the money he had saved and hidden where his father would not find it, and took the bus to State College. If he ever returned to Poplar Grove and St. Reg's none of us have seen him."

"He doesn't know how it ended?"

"We sent him copies of the tape. He may never have watched them."

Janie pushed the button again. We were in front of the old courthouse where county cases that pertain to Poplar Grove are heard. Don Silvio is surrounded by a group of his supernumeraries. Doña Mariana Pia, in a black pants suit, stands next to him, her blond hair in a severe ponytail and her steel eyes looking like weapons of mass destructon.

"Yesterday I asked the State's Attorney as a matter of personal friendship to determine the results of the blood-alcohol tests for Peter Kane, which the Poplar Grove police have been reluctant to reveal. I wanted to be sure that I was on solid ground before I began filing my motion. He called me just before midnight to report that he had gone to the police station here in Poplar Grove with a group of state police and removed by force the blood that was tested and the results of the test. I interviewed Mr. Kane and found that he had been severely beaten by the police. I ordered them to release him at once, which they did only this morning. I am entering motions this afternoon to hold Capt. Lee Elgin and the entire Poplar Grove police force in contempt of court for obstruction of justice. I am asking for a special prosecutor to investigate their dereliction of duty. I want the two cars in the accident impounded so that a qualified safety engineer can determine what actually happened. I demand that the files on the cameras in front of the nearby bank be impounded before the police destroy them; such vital evidence will leave no doubt what happened on that tragic night. I require that the two cars be examined for traces of alcohol and/or narcotics. I intend to file defamation suits this afternoon, naming Captain Elgin and the police force, Bellarmine high school president, Fr. Theobald, and the local province of the Society of Jesus in favor of my daughter Mariana Pia, whose good name has been irresponsibly and perhaps permanently harmed by their inappropriate comments. There will be similar suits against the various television channels that have defamed her and Mr. Kane—and myself in the process. I will pursue these actions with all my vigor and power. Lines have to be drawn against those who cheerfully defame the innocent only to obtain publicity for themselves. I do not represent Mr. Kane, but I will seek relief for him too."

"So what happened?" I asked Marty.

"He won a lot of money for Mariana and Pete, all of it in trust funds."

"I bet Mariana sandbagged them. She prepared her rant, tricked them into interviewing her and then dumped on them."

"She's a dangerous woman, Padre."

"Tell me about it! Then what happened?"

"Mariana went to Smith for three years to keep her mother happy and returned to law school," Marty said. "They had a big fight at home about taking on the police. Don Silvio decided in favor of his daughter. Pete earned his way through college by signing up for the ROTC. He's getting shot at in Iraq because this town and this parish let him down. I think he's wrong, but you gotta give him credit for integrity."

"I know he'll come back eventually," Jane insisted. "He still loves her. I just know that. She still cares."

"What do you want me to do?"

"Figure out something that will save them both."

I thought about it.

"I'll try."

Jane hugged me. Marty and I shook hands. They gathered up their tapes and left the monsignor's study—which was now *my* study.

15

Capt. Kane.

Fr. Jimmy. I hear it's Monsignor now.

Not to your old friends, Captain.

Such as they may be.

There seems to be a lot of them. I'm under constant pressure from them to do something about you.

Get me out of Iraq?

Not exactly.

I'll be redeployed again soon. I spent a lot of time this tour in a hospital bed.

No one will come after you with a sacred sword in there.

In this country you never can tell.

Are we winning the war like the government people say?

Hell, no. We'll never win here. It would have taken a half million soldiers at the beginning. The big brass weren't ready. No plans for after we took over, no armor, no nothing.

The brass don't read history books, do they?

That's why I'm getting a doctorate in history. I'll pick up the rest of my courses next time I'm home . . .

Here?

No, down in Texas, you should excuse the expression.

These friends of yours who are putting pressure on me . . .

Jane and Marty—

And others. They want you to spend some time here at St. Reg's this next time. . . . You still there, Pete?

Just being silent. I can't come home now, maybe not ever. I made a terrible mess of things. I'm still disgusted with myself. I ran. I was a coward.

No one would call you a coward anymore.

Different kind.

Most people wouldn't agree. Your side won. Selling the hotel was the thing to do. For a while.

I had good lawyers, didn't I?

That's the whole problem, isn't it, Pete?

Does she talk about me?

All the time.

She hates me?

No way. She's waiting for you.

She's a fool if she keeps waiting.

She'll wait forever.

Tell her not to.

Wouldn't do any good.

I've got a war on.

Doesn't bother her. You two still have an agenda.

Not after all these years.

Till judgment day you two will have an agenda. Maybe after.

I know that, Monsignor. I know that. Not now.

When?

Next time. I promise next time I'm redeployed, I'll show up at St. Reg's for a few days.

16

Mariana,

I have tried to write this letter many times during the last couple of years. I finish half of it and then delete it from the disk. I tell myself that I can finish it next time. Now on my third deployment to Iraq I realize that next time might be diminishing. I don't have any premonitions. I'm not expecting to die. I have been shot up twice and still managed to return to duty. My survival odds are still pretty good. Two men in my troop died this afternoon. Instantly. I have just finished letters to their families, parents in one case, wife and children in the other. I wonder if there were any unsent regrets in their minds as they stopped living. I wouldn't mind thinking of you at the end of my life, Mariana, the final step to heaven, but I wouldn't want anymore regrets that I could have expressed if I knew there would not be another next time. So I have sworn solemnly to myself that I will finish this letter and send it off to your new e-mail address at your law firm. You don't have to reply. I almost wrote "please don't reply," but that would perhaps have opened old wounds, which I do not want to do.

To begin with, congratulations on your graduation from college and the honors you received. Congratulations on law school and being editor of your school's law journal. Congratulations on the excellent job you have in a firm so high class that even I have heard of it.

There are people who love us both, you see, who want to keep me informed. I feel very proud of your achievements. I hear that you run the marathon. Even as a little girl you were faster than any of the guys. I mean "fast" in the good sense of the word!

People say that I'm a hero. I'm only doing my duty over here. But on the most important night in my life so far I wasn't a hero and I didn't even do my duty. I ran. And, damn it, Mariana! I'm still running. I ran away from my humiliation and from my father and from my guilt. My friends tell me that I am full of shit. Maybe I am. I don't know. I feel like I'm sinking into a swamp of self-disgust. That's all I know. There are many kinds of courage, Mariana Pia. This one I don't seem to have. I'd like to blame it on my father, but that wouldn't be right either.

Mariana, I've sat here staring blankly at this screen for a half hour. I think I'd better give up. But I'm not going to change a word. I'll tell you what Msgr. Jimmy and my old friends want me to say. I'll spend some time in Poplar Grove during my next redeployment. Perhaps we have an agenda after all. I won't run away this time.

Love,

17

My darling Pete,

I blubbered four straight hours after I read your beautiful letter. I won't ask who told you my e-mail address. Probably that wonderful busybody Jane Finn (who has the most beautiful little boy child, but you must know that too and have pictures of him). The trouble was that I had to discuss almost immediately with one of our faintly senile senior partners a draft of a petition he was about to enter in the appellate court here. It was a brilliant petition if I do say so myself, since I had written it. He wasn't so senile that he wanted to reject my work. He wanted to argue about matters of punctuation. So, being my father's daughter I grabbed all five style books that I have stored in my personal library here at the office and took him on. He yielded on most points and I conceded a few. He enjoyed it immensely. Arguably it was a form of sexual harassment, though he would have argued with a male assistant partner. He would not have enjoyed it so much, however.

At the end, having won his final point, because I was in a

good mood—one of my better moods in the last ten years—
he asked if he might ask me a personal question.

"So long as it is not too personal," I said.

"I wonder if the aura of happiness that surrounds you this
winter morning means you might be in love."

"I just might, sir."

"Might I offer congratulations?"

"Not yet, sir. We have a long agenda, but we've made some
progress recently."

"He's in Iraq?"

"Yes, sir, he's a captain in the First Cavalry."

"My old outfit. Will you tell him that, as one trooper to another,
he is a very lucky man."

"I certainly will."

Then I crept back to my cubicle and cried my happy heart
out. You have the moral advantage, dearest Pete, because
you took the first step and you had drafted many earlier letters
and had the opportunity to be careful with your words—always
necessary when dealing with a lawyer, even a lovesick one. I
will have to cry all day and for the rest of the night before I can
continue our discussion. But before I can consider my brief, let
me state my position about our agenda: I love you, I have always loved you, and I will always love you. Take care of yourself and come home to me this summer, your wonderful self.

Love, Mariana

How could have I forgotten how smart and funny and beautiful
she was.

I clicked on the REPLY button and wrote hastily:

My wonderful Mariana. The siren just sounded. There was
an explosion somewhere in town and we must go to the site
and see what happened. I'll write as soon as I get back.

I accept your agenda item. Even though I'm often what my poor mom calls an eejit, I feel the same way.

It won't be so long a time before I write another e-mail to my love.

Pete

18

It was another one of those scenes in which the Servants of God had slaughtered scores of God's children, Muslims like themselves. Two of them had driven a truck bomb into a school whose students were just emerging at the end of the school day. Another big victory for God. Blood and wreckage and torn bodies were all around us. Sirens were wailing. Orders were snapped in many languages. The air was thick with the smells of explosive and burning human flesh.

Our job was to seal off the square where Iraqi medics were picking up the bloody pieces and loading some of the kids who were still alive into ambulances. Another platoon was in the square itself trying to console the screaming parents, some of whom were blaming us for what had happened. I told my troopers to set up road blocks, fire warning shots over vehicles trying to violate the road blocks, and to take cover when a car seemed to be getting too close.

"Maybe, Captain sir," said PFC Kramer, a female trooper, "the people in the car will be looking for their kids."

"Maybe. But we have to protect our own and the survivors and ambulances. Don't fire until I give the order."

I daydreamed about Mariana. Her e-mail revealed in a few sentences her whole personality—funny, emotional, intelligent, loving. But it didn't reveal her paralyzing beauty. What an idiot I had been. I didn't deserve a second chance with her. But I was going to take it and make up for lost time.

Perhaps I daydreamed a little too long. A taxi raced around a corner, maybe seventy-five yards away. It ignored the ruined Fiat that was our road block and charged us. I stepped forward.

"Take cover!" I ordered. "Immediately!"

I fired a burst of automatic ordnance at him and he kept coming. I had seen suicide bombers attacking before. This one smelled of martyrs doing God's will. No time for a second thought. I fired at the engine block. The car swerved to a halt. He was going to martyr himself. I leaped behind the Fiat and found myself flying through the air in a blast of hot air and thick smoke.

Three strikes and you're out, I told myself and tried to say "Mariana!" I don't know whether I got the word out. And she'd never know either. I was only barely conscious on the street. PFC Kramer was kneeling next to me, saying the Hail Mary.

"Sorry, sir, you were right!"

I patted her hand. She smiled through her tears.

A couple of medics were kneeling around me. They were working on my battered and insanely painful body.

"We're losing him!"

"Captain Kane!" Kramer cried.

"It can't be! We can't lose him!"

Right. Peter Patrick Kane is indestructible.

I suddenly felt cold, as I often did cutting across Poplar Park on the way to St. Reg's. What had happened in that park, one spring night? I couldn't remember. But it was fun. Mariana! Then they were carrying me into a chopper that had dropped into the square.

"Pete Kane . . . 'Fraid he's gone!"

"Good God! No!"

I was outside the chopper, watching the whole thing.

"Damn it! I'm not gone. I'm still alive. I can hear you talking."

But I didn't feel pain anymore. Bad sign.

Then I was in the hospital again, laid out on one of their beds. Three doctors were pushing and poking at me.

"We can't let him die!"

"He's slipping away!"

"Stop the flow of blood!"

A woman's voice: "He's still breathing. Give him oxygen and more blood packs."

"We don't want to lose him!"

The woman was Sr. Joan Marie. What was she doing in Iraq?

"I don't want to lose me either," I said.

They never heard me.

I was twisting at an odd angle and then I left my bloody body behind and floated to the roof of the hospital tent. I watched with little interest as the doctors continued to struggle to stop my blood from spilling on the floor. Then they gave in and let me go. I was hurtling somewhere, carried by a presence of some sort—a friendly presence.

"You Gabe?" I asked.

"I'm his brother Rafe. Those are not our real names, but those are the ones humans use."

High-class angels. Nothing but the best for angelic little Petey Pat.

"Take care of Mariana for me, please."

"Don't worry, we will."

19

ANCHOR: We are told, Wendy, that there is a rumor in Baghdad that Capt. Peter Kane died today, killed by a suicide bomber.

EASTLAND: That seems to be true. A devout Roman Catholic, Capt. Kane was anointed by a priest in a helicopter that was taking him to the field hospital within the Green Zone. There is no confirmation yet. They will have to notify his next of kin first.

> Eastland makes no attempt to conceal her tears.

EASTLAND: I am speaking with Private First Class Carol Kramer, who was kneeling next to Capt. Kane when he was dying.

KRAMER: I had questioned him about firing on approaching cars that might have bombs. . . . You could always talk to Pete. Might some not be carrying parents rushing to see if their children were alive? He said that we had to protect the children inside the square who were still alive. He landed right next to me after the explosion blew him off the ground. You were right, sir, I said as I wept. He patted my hand and then he stopped breathing. I'll never forget him. I now realize how stupid this war is.

20

I am writing this account of my trip based on the tape I dictated on the flight to Ramstein to the flight nurses who are researching the phenomenon of soldiers injured by assaults on the brain in Iraq. They tell me that I am only somewhat unusual in reporting such experiences, though I show no evidence of concussion. I have also added details based on memories that arise as I read the tape. The main story and the conflict between God and myself are all on the original tape. I have also been steeping myself in the literature that Msgr. Jimmy brought over from Chicago along with his consistently good advice, with which I do not want to comply. Not yet anyway. I am also working on a rough draft memo that I am writing for Gen. Fred Rogers with my reflections on this stupid war. I do not consider myself a writer, though I did well in my assignments in high school and college. Now I can weave back and forth between two subjects when one or the other becomes high pressure.

I state here for the record in case something happens to me that my therapy, which takes five hours every day, is going well and my memory is almost normal, though I have a sense that there are some important matters that I have not tended to. Msgr. Jimmy is free with his suggestion that I am still hiding some major truths. I suppose he is right and I will have to agree with him eventually.

I have no sense of what time means in "the City," as it is called. (The City of God or has he stolen the name from St. Augustine?) My experiences in the City seem to occupy a considerable amount of time, though I was only in the "flat" period (which marks my kind of sustained and detailed experiences) for nine and a half minutes. They normally last no more than nine minutes, after which damage can occur to the brain. It seemed like it was much more, but there is no reason the One (the name they used up there—short, I am told, for One in Three) is constrained by time constraints.

One more observation, based on a distinction made by Prof. Zaleski. What happened to me in that "flat state" proves nothing about the existence of God or the issue of life after death. For me the contact with the Transcendent was unique and unquestionable. *I've been there. I know!*

For others it may be a hint, nothing more but nothing less.

The other question is the involvement of my brain. It was still in my body in the hospital in Baghdad. What happened to me in the City was somehow transferred or imprinted on my brain, perhaps as something like a videotape. As Collette told me those who live in the City are not ghosts, they are human persons who have bodies that will be bonded (her word) with our spirits permanently and completely in the time of the Parousia. Now the bonding wasn't quite complete but was good enough for a temporary arrangement.

I wasn't quite sure what that meant.

My trip from Baghdad to the City came to a smooth glide and then a firm stop.

"See you around, Petey Pat," my celestial taxi driver said gently.

"Thanks for the lift, Rafe," I replied.

I was standing on some sort of moving transparent bridge overlooking a large city, a glittering mixture of buildings large and small, a blend of familiar and unfamiliar architectural styles, though they were integrated one with another in attractive and sometimes astonishing combinations—perhaps by someone who didn't mind diversity, but insisted on good taste.

The homes and offices, or that's what I assumed they were, were multicolored, glowing pastels under a pale blue sky that made our blue sky look brutish. There were lots of parks in which the grass was deep, rich green, and little groves of tall trees that might have been redwood. Whoever the architects were they had chosen to create a science-fiction setting.

"Who designed this place, Rafe?"

I looked around but he was gone. Was he a regular on this route or was I getting some sort of VIP treatment?

"Is this supposed to be heaven or something?"

Whatever.

I continued to amble along the sky bridge. There was no evidence that I should be hurrying, so I took my time. Then quite suddenly I was outdoors. I detected an overwhelming scent and heard beautiful sound. The scent was of spring flowers and hence of flourishing life, a huge botanical garden, so sweet that it made me want to curl up and take a long nap. But I kept walking. What would happen when the tour was over? I wanted to see as much as I could of this astonishing City before I had to return home.

Home? Ft. Hood? Poplar Grove? Am I dead? Is this place heaven? If so, where's God? Are all these people dashing around on the streets down there—are they dead too? What's going on? Who are those folks on that balcony over there? They're waving at me and cheering. What have I done?

They're your relatives. They are very proud of you. They're welcoming you home. We try to have people here to greet our new arrivals.

The voice was familiar. Who is she? I turned around—Collette! But she was a mass of human wreckage when Neil Elgin's SUV crushed her. Now she was a beautiful woman in a maroon gown with a gold stripe down the front.

I hugged her and she hugged me back. She was definitely not a ghost and neither was I. Her face wasn't craggy, her hair wasn't straight and lifeless, her body wasn't lumpy, and she had learned how to smile.

You like the new Collette? The Angels remake us when we first arrive, because there is no ugliness in the City. They're such darlings. They insist that they are just undoing the mistakes nature made with us and the One doesn't like to be reminded how many mistakes he has made with us. He wants us to look like we should have looked.

The One is God?

We don't use that name around here. He's the One or the One in Three. Sometimes he's just the Boss. He laughs at that. He laughs a lot. If people in the Preparation World knew how much God laughs, they'd stop believing in him.

Three persons, really?

Really! Sometimes you can tell which one is talking to us. But often that doesn't worry you. The Greek theologians did a good job in trying to explain the Three in One, but there's a lot more work we have to do.

We?

I'm a theologian. Everyone chooses some kind of profession. You remember all the questions I used to ask poor Fr. Jimmy about God? Now I ask them with a lot of other people. We invite some of the most famous theologians to join us. I had a great argument with St. Augustine and St. Anselm the other day. They let me think I won! They're both so cute . . . Still the pushy Polack, huh, Petey Pat?

I never called you that.

I know. . . . Well, go on and ask your question about sex.

All right, what do you do for sex up here?

Well, we're still male and female, but we don't need to procreate because there is always a steady stream of new people coming in. Besides, that is a drag and we used to go crazy over it. So we don't fuck and we don't miss it. But there is something that's much better. We call it Oneness. We pause in what we're doing and give ourselves over completely to the goodness and affection of our companion. Then enormous charges of goodness stretch between us and our partner and we are filled with joy, almost as much as when we are in the presence of the Boss. But we don't have to invade his body, the soul is much more wonderful.

Joe is your companion?

Who else? He's up in the mountains climbing. When he comes home tomorrow we'll find a quiet and comfortable place either in our apartment or whatever and drink of each other's goodness and love. And there's no letdown afterward. And no jealousy or suspicion either. You can't beat it.

As we talked we strolled through the City, greeted the other people we met and joined them in a little song that was the song of the day, I was informed. My white tunic apparently identified me as a new arrival because I was warmly welcomed. I noticed that many of the couples we encountered seemed to be in an ecstatic trance. Or maybe they were simply consumed by the love between them.

We crossed a little park filled with lilac bushes and approached a small house whose door opened. A large wolfhound-like creature bounded out the door and embraced Collette like he had not seen her for years.

Boris is a Polish wolfhound. In the City there are pets for those in whose lives they played important roles.

She and Joe lived in a small but comfortable house that looked very much like the modest bungalow in which the Worskis lived back in St. Regis. Probably the angels were responsible for that—knickknacks on every available flat space, lace doilies on the arms of the chairs, dark, heavy furniture. She directed me to a plush easy chair into which I sank immediately.

Long trip, Pete?

I think so.

And that explosion was powerful?

She knew that I was in principle dead. But then she was too. As were most everyone in this imposing and colorful city.

Will I see Joey?

He won't be back till late.

He's as happy here as you are?

Of course, we're all happy. We are not trapped in original sin anymore, which in fact is fear of our own mortality. Take away that fear and we can relax, no need to be stressed, no envy or jealousy, nobody to fight with, competition, but no conflict—what we could have been on earth if we weren't so afraid. And we have the One taking care of us and loving us like a doting father, which of course is what he is.

Everyone gets in here?

We don't know for sure. We theologians go back and forth on it. I argue that the One loves each of his children so much that he won't let them go, even if they try to get away. Lee Elgin is around here, though ashamed to talk to Joey and me. So I guess he managed to get in. The One has talks with each of us when we arrive and we straighten things out. Some people find it very difficult but others love to say how neat the One is.

You find God to be "neat"?

Totally. There are probably stages one has to grow through to be admitted and even after they get in, they seem to have to work at it. It's all kind of private, so we don't ask any questions. The One told me that I was lucky to have a priest like Fr. Jimmy who didn't try to scare us with God . . .

Is this the only City?

We like to speculate on that. We don't see any Neanderthal people around here and I'm sure the One loves them as much as he loves us. Occasionally there are strangers wandering in the main square. We are polite to them and they to us, but it would be rude to ask them whether they're from the Bronze Age.

So should I worry about my session with him after you're through with me?

I was honored to welcome you and to tell you how wonderful the City is.

I'm sorry, I apologize. I guess I'm not quite free of original sin. She smiled.

I never thought you had much of it, Petey Pat, except when you ran out on poor Mariana.

Well you have to admit that she is a woman to be afraid of.

That's her mother. Mariana is a cupcake.

You have a lot of church services around here? You must have to worship the One intermittently?

We worship him all the time by our work and play and love. We have some special days of worship we all attend to celebrate his wonderful work for us. No rules. Worship is part of being fully human. . . . You know that, Petey—Fr. Jimmy taught us, didn't he?

So the One is a he?

As Cardinal Cusa said centuries ago, in God all opposites are combined. So God is both male and female and neither male nor female. Sometimes it seems to me that the One shifts back and forth.

One last question: How do I find a companion before Mariana joins us?

The One will discuss her with you.

Free of original sin, she could still evade my questions deftly. The One had chosen my first reactor wisely.

She rose from her couch, disappeared into the back of their cottage and returned with two cookies and a flask of some purple liquid. I was being dismissed.

At the other end of this park the Great Forest begins. You go through the gate and down the path and the Three in One will meet you on it. Do not be afraid. You are loved more than you love. By the way, there's a small lake maybe a mile into the forest. You may swim in it if you wish. The One will not interfere in your privacy.

How will I recognize him?

You won't have any trouble.

She hugged me and kissed me gently, and I left, dizzy with affection.

We will meet again, Petey Pat. Give my love to Mariana.

21

I arrived at the gate into the Great Forest, dazed and riding an emotional high. Everything was so beautiful. Collette was still alive. She had forgiven me. She loved me despite her death. The music from the City continued, as did the singing. The environment—trees, flowers, bushes, grass—were not quite like those on earth, but they were lovely. The breeze was light. I did not mind being dead, though I was not sure that I was really dead. The lunch—cookies and the purple drink—were energizers, as was Collette's farewell. She was a beautiful, intelligent, and irresistible woman. I loved her, yet in that love there was no hint of the lust I would have felt if our encounter had been on earth.

I had learned a lot about the City and the One who presided over it. I would do my best to remember it all so I could describe it to Mariana when I returned home.

Except this was home now, wasn't it?

I wrestled with my questions as I consumed the cookies and the magic potion. I didn't know that it was a *magic* potion, but why not? This was all a dream, wasn't it? I was still in the field hospital, in a coma, still barely alive. I pushed through the gate and entered the magic forest. It had to be magic, or at least artificial. The tall trees, something like pines perhaps, filtered the sunlight that burnished the soft, wild-flowered path that wound through the forest. There were no stones on the path and no undergrowth in the forest.

Was any of it real?

Probably not. Everything was too perfect, too clean, too neat, too beautiful. It was all an illusion. Maybe I was fantasizing as I lay dying. I was temporarily in a dream world—something like the one that led the jihadist martyrs to detonate themselves and everyone else in sight. The women were all beautiful, just as Islam promised they would be, though most of them were not virgins, but inaccessible because they were partnered with lifelong companions. Would priests and nuns have partners? What was the sense of celibacy in heaven?

And what about those who had remarried after death or divorced? Didn't Jesus say that there was no marriage, or giving in marriage, in heaven? Or did he mean that there was no economic function in marriage like there had been? Or did a gendered relationship that did not involve intercourse not fall under that rule?

And how did they get rid of garbage in the City, or human waste? Or was I an idiot for asking such questions? Wasn't it enough to know that there was a world to come, a place were God's love was in charge? Or was this all a reverse nightmare on a slab in Baghdad? If it was a dream, it couldn't last much longer, could it?

Then I came upon the little lake that Collette had promised—deep blue, smooth, inviting. What was there to lose? I dipped my foot into the water. Pleasant enough. I shed my caftan and dove in and swam vigorously, hoping that the water and the exercise would clear my head. The warmth of the lake and its scent soothed my nerves and calmed me down but I found no answers to my questions. I had better go down the forest path and face my particular judgment with my Maker, who probably had many scores to settle.

I climbed out of the lake and donned my caftan, which of course absorbed the moisture from my body. However, as I was pulling it over my head, I noticed that the body was not mine. The angels who had put together a body for me had made a mistake. The scar from the Persian sword was gone.

So!

Yeah, but what did that mean? The One had a lot of questions to answer.

The sun was beginning to set, sinking behind the trees and painting the sky a delicate rose. Nice effect!

Then I was aware that there was someone on the path with me. I was absorbed by a powerful emotion, one that had never affected me back on earth, should this world be distinct from earth. I tried to grasp the emotion. It had to be love. I was in the presence of an overwhelming love from which it would be impossible to escape. Was this what the catechism had meant by the beatific vision?

Then I was enveloped by a dazzling white cloud, glowing with ever-changing rainbow lights.

" 'Tis Yourself," I said.

" 'Tis . . . and who else would it be?"

The voice was amused, gentle, affectionate. Neither male nor female, but both male and female and delighted with me.

"And you ask a lot of questions, don't you?"

"Can I ask one more?"

"I don't see why not. But I know what it is already—how do I account for the problem of evil? Why do good people suffer and die?"

"And also why do I think I can do anything I want?"

The One was caressing me tenderly, like I was a newborn babe, which I suppose I was.

"Well, that's a second question."

"You have to answer the first one."

"Indeed I do. I have to answer it eventually to everyone who asks. But, you see, Petey Pat, it's not the right question."

"And that is . . ."

I was certainly disrespectful. This was the Alpha and the Omega, the beginning and the end, and I was acting like a smart-ass high school sophomore. Or a First Communion candidate.

"Why would anyone think that it is possible to create a perfect world, programmed from the first instant to produce thinking and loving creatures?"

"I never thought of it that way."

"It was a single explosion, one big bang that's still going on and you expect it to be a perfect world. I had to battle nature with all its mathematical laws and its uncertain algorithms to produce anything at all. No one ever did it before, don't you see, so there was no hope of making it perfect. It's a lot better than it might have been and I'm slowly bringing it under control—with the help of humans, I might add. Then if you're going to have humans in this creation, you introduce a lot more problematics."

"I thought you could do anything you wanted. Aren't you om-nipotent?"

"Have I ever claimed to be omnipotent?"

"I'm not a Protestant. I can't quote scripture."

The sound he made was more like an exasperated sigh than a laugh.

"I assure you that I have not. The problem with this problem of evil bit is that everyone thinks I can do anything I want. You should have learned better in second grade. Your teacher taught you that God can't do contradictions, right?"

"Sr. Joan Marie?"

"Remarkable woman. One of my favorites. What did she tell you?"

"That's easy. God can't make a square circle. It's a contradiction."

"So is a perfect cosmos, a nature that can't make any mistakes."

"So your power is limited?"

"Sure I am, but only within the context in which I'm working, and the context was and is very intractable and a stubborn human nature. I have to respect the freedom of both and still achieve my goals. So I made this place where I can dry the tears of all my injured children. I think on balance it was still a good idea to create. I'll win in the end—and so will all my children."

There was not a touch of impatience in his tone as he tried to explain.

"Are you surprised that it has taken so long?"

"What makes you think it's been long?"

"You took an awful chance, didn't you?"

"That's why there has to be a God. It's his job to take chances."

"You know you will win in the long run, don't you?"

"You know St. Paul?"

"Heard of him, never met him."

Then the trees shook and the ground rocked. The laughter of God is a mighty thing.

"Well, he said that I emptied myself to become human. Jesus was my second big gamble. I'm winning that one too. But it isn't easy."

"Why did you bother?"

"You gotta do something."

He began to laugh. He laughed through most of the rest of the conversation. "You think you have a crazy God on your hands?"

"It is what it is."

"But it's getting better."

"So far, I haven't been much of a help, have I?"

"As your Irish ancestors would say, you're not the worst of them."

"Sorry about that."

He roared with laughter.

"When you get back you'll write about this experience. You must tell them that God laughs a lot. God is a Deus Jocoso."

"I am not going back and I won't write about this place."

"Yes, you will. All those years at State U when you drowned yourself in history books in a useless attempt to forget about the love of your life, you dreamed of being an author. So you will write about this place. It's all right with me, so long as you let people know that I laugh a lot. Now, let's get on with your record."

"I thought we'd left that behind."

More laughter this time, I assumed over my evasions.

"First, there's your father . . ."

"I shouldn't have knocked him down . . ."

"I didn't say that. You were protecting yourself and your family. My problem is that you should have tried to reconcile with them afterward. They've all changed. Your mother is more in control. Your father has chilled out. He joined AA and stopped drinking to pray to me to bring you back alive. Your little sisters are growing into strong and delightful young women. You haven't given them a second chance. They're very proud of you—your father especially."

"Does it help now to say that I'm sorry and acted like an eejit?"

"Of course it helps. You were dealt a weak hand of cards. You might have killed the poor man, if it hadn't been for my friend Mariana. And then you walk out on her."

"Well, I did send those e-mails to her."

"Only at the last minute, and I had to overwhelm you with grace so you'd do it."

"At least I went along with your grace while there was still time, didn't I?"

"At the last possible minute. I don't blame you for getting out of town. They made life impossible there. But you could have at least talked to her on the phone, couldn't you? You know very well that you are the love of her life."

"I didn't know that."

"Yes, you did, but you have been and are too afraid of her to even talk to her—and have been for seven years."

He continued to laugh.

"Not exactly afraid of her."

"Who am I?"

"The Lord my God is, I think, one of the titles you use."

For the first time in our dialogue there was a touch of exasperation in the One's voice.

"If I say you're afraid of her, you are afraid of her."

"OK."

"What displeases me, insofar as I am able to be displeased, is that you are more afraid of her than of me. She is a beautiful and gifted young woman and would scare most men, but I am, as you say, the Lord your God."

"What am I supposed to do now?" I asked.

"You are supposed to go back to earth and give yourself to Mariana and accept herself in return."

"No way!"

"You realize that your real body has been brain-dead for seven and a half minutes. If you are to go back, we must not waste time."

"Fine, I'll wait up here—if 'up' is the right word—until she joins us and then the two of us will be happy together for all eternity."

"No, you won't!"

"Why not?"

"You were destined to be her lover, but you ran away. Mariana needs a lover and a protector. If you don't claim her, she will marry someone else."

"Who!" I demanded.

"Whom. That is none of your business just now. He will be a good husband—not as good as you would have been, but she will love him. And she will swim with him in that lake you enjoyed so much."

"What's so special about her?"

"Once every couple of centuries, Peter Patrick Kane, someone emerges from the sea of faces I see who has the capability of redirecting part of human history. Mariana is one of those. I checked the scenario we had developed for her life. She needed a special kind of mate. There you were, the perfect match. We don't manipulate people into their marital choices, but there was no doubt from the first time you saw each other that such a marriage was made in heaven, quite literally. Then you blew it . . . not when you left St. Reg and Poplar Grove, but when you ruled her out of your life."

We reached the end of the forest and I climbed the hill that waited for us. The great, shining and irresistible glob of light kind of shimmered up the hill.

"But I ruled her *back* into my life!"

"One final piece of advice about your book. The skeptics will be all over you. This place, they will say, was an illusion created by the memories in your brain as chemicals poured in to protest against death. You've dreamed this whole place . . . including these playing fields."

At the top of the hill we looked over a vast plain in which every sport I know was in action—men's teams, women's teams and mixed teams. At the bottom of the hill were dozens of games in which teams kicked footballs around. I saw no American football games.

"No Notre Dame?"

"Too rough."

"No NFL?"

"We don't have enough angels to repair the injured."

"They must be dull games. If everyone is in perfect condition, there's no competition, is there?"

Just beneath us two women's teams were engaged in a fearsome sport that might have been soccer but wasn't quite. The players were dressed in modest blouses and shorts, but since women by definition are attractive they were a delight to watch.

"People here are in good health but they don't lose their natural talents. My good friend Tiger will always be the best golfer in history."

"I notice"—more laughter—"that you appreciate the loveliness of the women in that game. Which brings us back to Mariana Pia."

"The answer is still no."

More laughter.

"You sound less confident now that you know that someone else will have her for all eternity."

"That's not funny."

"You know her after all those years almost as well as I do. You will not give her up."

"Yeah?"

He was right, of course, and he knew it. I was just being stubborn because it is in my nature to be stubborn.

"Chance intrudes into some of our most carefully cultivated scenarios. Then we have to intrude to cancel out the effects of chance. We have been watching you very carefully. When it became clear that you were really going to die in that explosion, we brought you up here. We want you to return not only for her sake but also for your own. I can't force you to return to her. I will be disappointed if you don't, but I will still love you."

"I'm terrified of her."

"Naturally, but you have learned much since you saw her last, and our special grace will be with you."

"I won't know what to do."

"Yes, you will. Petey Pat, you love her. She loves you. And I love both of you. I'll talk like a Chicagoan: Do me a favor. Go back and love her the way that only you can."

"All right," I said. "But you owe me a marker."

"Gabe!" He summoned the messenger. "Do some basic repair work on this person while you're delivering him."

"Glad to, Boss."

"One last bit of advice, Pete. The skeptics will try to tear you apart. Tell them that you don't know what happened, but that you had an ecstatic experience when you discovered that there was a part of you that was open to life everlasting, and then you encountered the One who would respond to that experience. You suppose that your life experiences colored your description of what the other world is like."

"This is all illusion? These games? Collette? You?"

"It's all real, but necessarily it is colored by the images your brain has collected during your life."

"Whatever."

"You will have a sign that this is all real," Gabe said in a gentle tenor voice, suitable for startling a maiden in Bethlehem. "The real here is even better than what you've seen."

"See you later, Petey Pat," the One said as Gabe began to move me. "You can tell herself—but only if she asks."

God's voice was choked up. But Jesus wept at the tomb of Lazarus, didn't he?

"We're all chained by the bonds of love, aren't we?"

God's final words as I sped off on a trip from heaven to Poplar Grove were appropriate.

"Tell me about it!"

22

EASTLAND: Gen. Fred Rogers has scheduled a news con-
ference here at the headquarters of the American Army
in Iraq. We assume that it is to confirm the death of
Capt. Peter P. Kane, who was fatally wounded while
diverting a suicide bomber from a square in Baghdad.

ROGERS: Most of you have heard the report that Capt.
Pete Kane was killed by a suicide bomber yesterday.
That report was true. Capt. Kane expired at 2000
hours last night. However, nine and a half minutes
later he began to breathe again. Col. Dwight Schloss-
man, chief of brain surgery, has told me that while
such revivals are not uncommon, the length of the flat-
line on Capt. Kane's brain monitor was unusually
long. He himself has never observed such a period of
brain inactivity in his field, but he has read reports of

such phenomenon. We are delighted that Capt. Kane remains with us. His condition is still described as critical but he seems to be improving rapidly.

EASTLAND: I want to assure WTN watchers that I am not the only one in this room who is crying.

23

"Brain activity!" Nurse Crane shouted.

You'd better believe it, I thought.

"Farewell," Gabriel said. "Nice to meet you. We'll see you again, but not for a long time. You're in pretty good shape, considering."

"Give my best to the maid from Bethlehem!"

"I will . . . she's very interested in your case."

I watched my medical team, utterly unprepared for this phenomenon, panic. I smiled contentedly. This would be fun.

I twisted back into my body and opened my eyes.

"Vital signs all approaching normal," Nurse Crane sobbed.

"Good morning folks," I said. "Nice to be with you again."

Later Gen. Rogers appeared.

"They tell me you have no right to be alive, Pete."

I smiled blandly.

"I guess I owe someone a favor."

I was groggy from the painkillers they had shot into me. I

needed them, but the pain was not all that bad. Gabe must have done a good job on the trip down—if that was the right direction.

"What are the names of the Chicago sports franchises?"

"Da Cubs, Da Bears, Da Bulls, Da Blackhawks, Da Wolves."

"One more."

"I don't count the White Sox. . . . Oh, you mean da fightin' Irish. I guess they're so bad now that it's all right to add them to the list."

The scars had faded from my body. There was a slight hint of a wound where a rifle bullet had nicked my shoulder. And a thin white line on my left side where the ceremonial sword had invaded me was the only hint of the scar I had when I had left the Green Zone to establish a perimeter around the site of the truck bombing. The One wanted there to be a reminder that I really had spent some time in the City, if only nine and a half minutes—plus the trips back and forth, which probably required no more than a few seconds. If the passage of the years should dim my memory of the overwhelming love and the radiant beauty and the laughter of a laughing God, then I could check the traces of the once-ugly scars.

"You're going to learn to walk all over again. Do you want to go home to do that? Hines Hospital out in Elmwood? I hear it is on overload. How about Ramstein? The rehab facilities there are the best we have. You might want to re-enter the world there. Your family could come to visit you. There's no need to return home a cripple. You're a VIP now and you'll get VIP treatment."

"I don't want any special treatment."

"You'll get special treatment whether you want it or not."

"Yes, sir."

"I'll see to the logistics and be back to you in a day or two."

"Yes, sir."

I'm the kind of fraud who will argue with the Lord my God and won't argue with a two-star general.

He turned to leave.

Then he asked, casually, as though it were a second thought, "You didn't do any specially traveling while you were unconscious, did you?"

"Why do you ask, sir?"

"We've noticed that some of those who have had your kind of trauma report on one of these NDEs—near-death experiences. I assume you didn't?"

"Is this confidential, sir?"

"Absolutely. Some of our people are trying to study these NDE things. They're not sure how to react to them. All records will be kept strictly confidential."

My wit, which had caused me so much trouble on the school yard at St. Reg's came back.

"Nothing special, Gen. Rogers, sir. I visited heaven for a few minutes and had an argument with God. He won. Naturally. But he enjoyed arguing with me. So I came back here with an assignment. God has a great sense of humor. I thought that some day I might write about it . . . call the book *To Heaven and Back.*"

"That would be different from the book you're going to write for the Command School."

"*A Quick and Easy War?* I had kind of forgotten about that."

"Do you have any proof of your trip?"

"I will never doubt it, sir. I can't expect others to take my word for it."

"That's a common enough reaction, Pete. But let's say that I'm one of those skeptics. Convince me."

"I'm sure the doctors told you that I'm making remarkable progress. Bouncing back quickly. Good genes or something like that . . ."

He nodded, his face expressionless.

"You remember my scar from the Persian sword?"

He nodded again.

"It was pretty ugly. I didn't pay much attention to it. Every once in a while there was a little infection and the docs shot me up with antibiotics that ruined my appetite. When I took my shower the morning of my encounter with the jihadists, I thought it looked like another infection was brewing."

I lifted my hospital gown.

"Aw gone," I said, mimicking the voice of a kid.

"My God!"

"Actually, up there—though I won't swear to the accuracy of the preposition—they call him the One, or sometimes when they're being formal, they call him the One in Three. I'm not sure of the pronoun. I have the impression that God is neither male nor female *and* both male and female."

He nodded yet again.

"Now I'll be looking forward to two of your books. A psychologist will stop by to talk to you. Carry on, Captain."

He wanted to get away from me as quickly as he could.

I was proud of myself. The old Petey Pat was back.

Thank you, I murmured to the One. Sorry I was such a pain.

24

"Good evening, Captain Kane. I'm Dr. Cindy Irving."

"Shrink."

"Even better. A lieutenant colonel."

I opened my eyes. Middle thirties, dark hair, dark eyes, competent. Sexy in an understated way in her thick glasses and doctor's scrubs.

"I'll be flying to Ramstein with you."

"You'll tell them when to use restraints?"

"Every indication is that you are a rational, if very brave, man."

"Only problem is that I claim to have joked with God after an Iraqi suicide bomber killed me."

"An unusual claim, you must admit. Whatever my personal opinion on such phenomena may be, you will understand that my professional obligation is to be skeptical about your story."

"If I hadn't been there, I'd be skeptical."

"I have here," she opened her green manila folder, "a picture of a wound from a saber you acquired in your last deployment. It apparently has healed slowly."

She showed me another picture.

"Looks like me," I said, "but it was a sacred ceremonial sword from Persia. The late owner didn't claim it, so I liberated it."

"What was he like?"

"Big guy with a beard and a turban and wild eyes filled with hate. He thought a skinny little guy like me would be a pushover. He was astonished when I killed him, poor fellow."

She nodded, perhaps wondering what kind of nut I was.

"May I, uh, see that scar?"

"Sure it's not much anymore. I was looking forward to showing it off when I'm back home, if I ever make it there."

I lifted the gown again, more modestly this time. No exhibitionist, this Peter Kane.

"I see. You believe that this scar was healed while you were in, uh, heaven?"

"I don't know. I noticed only when I regained consciousness here. The One told Gabriel when he was getting ready to bring me back to spiff up some of my problems. I think you'd have to interview him for all the details."

"The voice of God . . . the only angel who can speak Caldee and Syriac."

"Gifted guy, I guess. The one who removed me from my body said he was Rafe, Gabe's brother, though those were not their real names."

"So you're telling me, Captain, that the Angel Gabriel, the one who visited the maid in Bethlehem, healed your scar on your voyage down from heaven."

"I didn't say that. I said that's a possibility. You'd have to interview him."

"You didn't ask him about the maid of Bethlehem?"

"No, I asked his brother on the way up. By the way, the 'up' and 'down' propositions are not literal. I don't know where the City is."

"And Rafael said about the maid . . . ?"

"Kid, child . . . I said she must have been something else. He said that was what his brother told him. Pushy Jewish mother."

She frowned as though I had said something politically incorrect. Which I had deliberately.

"Cana, St. John's Gospel, third chapter."

Dr. Irving blushed and smiled slightly.

"Not the last one."

From then on we were friends.

At the end of our first session I started to fade away.

"I'll talk to you on the flight to Ramstein."

She stood up, about to leave.

"Hey, I get this tape when you're finished with it."

"And a transcript for you to approve. See you in the morning. I'll bring a supply of straightjackets."

"Yeah, would you go to my quarters and collect my laptop and my cell phone?"

"Of course."

"Also there's a photo in the bottom drawer of my desk. Liberate that for me too."

"Certainly."

So Petey Pat was back, performing in the school yard and winning people over by his outrageous wit and his charm. Where had he been? Why had he been away so long?

25

Mariana Pia Elizabeta Angelina was wearing a black suit, no makeup or jewelry, and her most somber face.

"Msgr. Jimmy, I want to contribute a thousand dollars to some worthy missionaries to say two Masses for him every month for a year. Don't tell me that it is old-fashioned. I want to have holy men praying for him."

"It is not old-fashioned and it never will be, Mariana Pia, to make offerings to missionaries and ask for their prayers. I know of Irish missionaries who minister to AIDS victims in Africa. They will be very grateful for your generosity."

She gave me her check.

"You will write in their name and send it off to the family?"

"Certainly."

"I talked to Mrs. Kane. They will ship his body home by air and they will bury him at Most Holy Guardian Angels after a requiem Mass here. She will make arrangements with you as soon as they know when the body will arrive. She is very brave. His father has been crying since the announcement was on WTN."

"That's the way of it with the Irish," I said. "Our women folk try to hide their emotions and our men collapse."

"It is the opposite with us."

"Your mother?"

"The bitch doesn't try to hide her satisfaction. After he's buried, I will want to talk to you about my own future."

The phone rang. I'd better answer it. I'd need time to figure out what to say next.

"Jimmy . . . Yes, Mrs. Kane . . . Are you sure? Gen. Rogers confirmed it? He will recover? A Miracle indeed? She's here. I'll put her on."

I slipped out of my office to leave those two stalwart women a chance to weep their tears of joy in privacy.

What the hell was going on? Three strikes and he should have been out. We had better get him back here as soon as we could. Indeed his pastor, a man not without some high connections, should fly to Ramstein Air Force Base and make sure the young man was being treated with appropriate diligence.

The army fouled up many things routinely, like the Catholic Church. It even made mistakes about casualties. But Capt. Kane was one of the few authentic heroes of this misbegotten war. What could one conclude? Pete Kane had actually died on the operating table and then had been revived. Had he done anything in the meantime?

I called American Airlines and asked for the schedule from

Chicago to Frankfurt Airport, about seventy-five miles, if I remembered correctly, from Ramstein.

Pete Kane would come home with enough stories to last a couple of lifetimes.

26

The four prop-jet engines on the C-130 Hercules turned over lazily. The plane, perhaps forty years old, carried the insignia of the 86th Airlift Wing. Despite its age and bedraggled interior, it was the perfect model for a flying hospital. Most of us were destined for the Air Force Hospital at Ramstein, not quite in bad enough condition to merit transport to a hospital in the United States— if there were any military hospitals that were functioning well back home. But we were the sick or injured who needed better care than the field hospital in Baghdad could provide.

I didn't fit in either category. I had been killed in action and then had returned in surprisingly good condition. There was still a possibility that I might turn up with some form of brain-trauma stress syndrome. Gen. Rogers wanted me out of country because he considered me a strong investment in the future. The doctors who had treated me were afraid to have me around for fear that my recovery might reverse itself and they could be blamed. The

Pentagon probably wanted me in a place where I would get less attention than I would on the ground in Baghdad. Lock him up in Ramstein before he embarrasses us again.

Lt. Col. Cindy Irving climbed up the ramp to the flying hospital, glanced around anxiously to make sure that I hadn't slipped away for a return trip to the City, and smiled faintly when I feigned hiding from her under a pillow.

"You would drive the young woman crazy, Peter Patrick. As well as the Lord your God."

"He seemed to enjoy my company."

"Here is your rosary, your cell phone, appropriately recharged, your laptop, and your photograph, closed as I found it."

"You didn't look at it?"

"I assumed that it was private."

"Some things are private and yet designed to be looked at. It's herself at thirteen on an eighth grade class picnic."

She opened the leather case and swallowed. My love was wearing a white sweatshirt and cutoff jeans. Laughing.

"That's Mariana in her girl-athlete modality. She has many different modalities. The operative one now is doubtless Portia at the bar."

"Were you engaged?"

"Sure, we promised in kindergarten that we would marry when we grew up. The thing is that I never grew up."

"You lived with her?"

"No, I wouldn't be here if I'd done that."

"You slept with her?"

"Not for lack of desire."

"And your story," she flipped open her notebook, "is that the

God-person sent you back to take care of her? She doesn't look like she needs any protection."

"Which of us doesn't?"

"You still love her?"

"Certainly. The God-person laughed in my face when I said I might be no longer in love with her."

"And she loves you?"

"On the basis of one exchange of e-mail, she seems to."

"You are confident that you can woo her and win her?"

"Hell, no. But the God-person laughed at me when I said that."

"So you will go home and propose to her?"

I hesitated.

"I'll be scared."

"Any man would be." She tapped the leather case.

"I'll say something like, 'Mariana, we've been engaged for twenty years. Don't you think it's about time we invest in a marriage bed— a big one at that?'"

Though I was sedated and tranquilized, I felt my stomach muscles tighten. What if she turned me down cold . . .

The big propellers on the Hercules began to spin more rapidly. Their low buzz slowly shifted to a loud whine.

"When was this e-mail exchange?"

"Just before I died. I got her response to my first letter the day I blew up the suicide bomber. I can't remember whether I responded. I think—or maybe I hope—that I sent her a brief reply."

"She would have been very much on your mind when you took on that bomber."

The Hercules lumbered out to the runway like a turtle would have waddled into the Pacific before setting sail for New Guinea.

"I'm an Irish Catholic romantic, Dr. Cindy. I tried to whisper her name."

"So I put it to you that she was vividly on your mind when you died?"

" I suppose so."

"Then you encounter a God-person who orders you to return to take care of her and protect her. You disagree, but he insists."

The C-130 braked at the end of the runway. The pilot gunned the motors up one by one, as they do with prop planes before taking off. The demons in hell could not have cried out more horribly. Then he released the brakes and turned the plane around, spinning it almost on a dime. I shut my eyes; it was time to sleep. Maybe we'd crash and I could return to the heavenly city. I didn't want to be there if Mariana wasn't with me. The plane trundled down the runway, resisting with all its weight and mass the impulse to leave the ground. Then it seemed to rise a couple of inches, hesitate, and then with one last mighty heave hurled itself into the air.

My drugged dreams were peaceful. Then I woke up with a start and said, "Next question?"

"Were you sexually aroused when Collette kissed you good-bye?"

"No."

"Or in the lake when you were thinking of swimming there with Mariana?"

"I don't think so."

"Or when the God-person absorbed you?"

"If I were, I wouldn't have noticed it."

"No sexual arousals at all?"

"Not as such. I remember checking out the women who milled

through the streets and the squares and in the parks. They all had wonderful figures in their colorful caftans, all different—or so it seemed—but all interesting. There may have been a lot of love over there and it was gendered love but not lust . . . That doesn't make sense, but then I'm not a jihadist."

"You never saw Mariana?"

"How could I? She wasn't dead."

"Do you accept my suggestion that it was to be expected that in your final minutes you would fantasize about Mariana?"

"Sure."

"Yet you insist that it was a real experience and not a dream experience."

"It was both, Cindy. Obviously I was not in the real world I knew on earth. But it was real just the same, fantastically real. Nor were the images like those in any of the dreams and nightmares I've had or my daydreams either. It was all very lovely but strange too."

"And you don't read SF books?"

"Not yet. I'll start reading them."

"Do you dream now about the City?"

"Sure. All the time. My imagination is filled with pictures. I'm not sure, but I may be creating new pictures, filling in the blanks in my memory. I don't think I'm distorting anything . . ."

"But then you run the risk of distorting when you create pictures with your words. Have you drawn any of your images?"

"A few of them."

"Might I see some of them?"

"They're in the briefcase under my bed."

"Very interesting, Peter. They are appropriate for the world you describe in your text. When you publish your story you should insist that they include some of these."

"I can polish them up . . ."

"You should do that. But keep the originals. They are the closest to the events themselves . . . Collette is a darling young woman. But none of Mariana?"

"I'm sure she's in my dreams but I can't download her."

"These drawings confirm my own images, Pete—you paint with words and with a pencil the same reality. Your Deus Jocoso conveys the same impression as the text. I'm sure, should he be, he would not object."

"Which doesn't make him real."

"Only consistent."

"Precisely. I will report along with the text of the interview that you are well within the normal limits of mental health and that in fact the experience seems in general to have been functional for your mental health. While it was longer than most NDEs it was richer in details. It would be helpful if someone interviewed you in a couple of years. You were a religious person before the experience and are more religious now. Typically of those who have had these experiences you are less afraid of death than of proposing marriage. Your desires for women are healthy and on the whole respectful. Did you really have a brief interlude in the hereafter? Your prompt return to health, save for your battered legs, minimally suggest an unusual resilience. The virtual disappearance of your scars is not inconsistent with your claim of temporary experience of transcendence—spell that with a small or large T. I'll append this to the transcript."

"They'll conclude that I'm ready to return to combat."

"That bothers you?"

"Not really."

"If they do, they're out of their minds."

She bent over and brushed her lips against mine.

"At some point, Petey Pat, I'd love to see your drawing of me in the swimming lake with you. So, I'm sure, would my husband."

"Witch," I murmured. "That's with a 'W.'"

She kissed me again.

My early days at Ramstein were painful as the therapists pushed me hard to recover control of my legs. They wanted me to walk out of there as though my fall after the blast had not broken my legs. In truth they had healed nicely, another tribute to Gabe's therapy on my ride home. But these therapists wanted perfection. So for that matter did I. Mariana's children did not deserve a gimpy father, right? I also spent a fair amount of time in the pool. I continued to edit the transcript of my interlude in the City, so that it would be the first draft for the book I was going to write. Then at the end of the day I would turn to my favorite task, sketches of the City—penciling new ones and revising the old.

People would want to know whether that was what heaven was like. I would say that those were the images that had locked themselves into my highly subjective memory. The point was that heaven was a place of joy, happiness and challenge presided over by a jocose God who was pure love and pure mercy. Read the New Testament if you don't believe that.

The days blurred together, like summer camps with the ROTC. I ate huge amounts of food, put on weight and filled out the skinny places in my body. I had not realized the ravages that combat, strain and stress had taken on my organism. I was a child again striving to grow up.

The local shrinks kept watching me for any sign of PTSS—post-traumatic stress syndrome—a big deal these days. A few of them wanted to challenge Cindy Irving's diagnosis. I had, however, learned how to play the game of fending off shrinks, especially the reductionist kind.

The most frequent question was whether I wanted to return to combat. My standard answer was that no one in his right mind wanted to redeploy to Iraq after three years of combat and three Purple Hearts. But I had taken an oath of allegiance to my commanders and I would go back if they wanted to send me there. They thought they had me both ways. If I said that I would go back then I was out of my mind. If I said I wouldn't they'd write me up as mutinous and just a little crazy. Fortunately most of the team that was on my case thought that I had some crazy ideas, but was still a good soldier and a brave and resourceful officer.

I was walking back from the pool to my quarters—which were bigger than those in Iraq—to begin my writing for the day. I had dominated the school yard for years at St. Reg's because of my ability to tell stories. I had no trouble doing term papers in high school, as tongue-tied as I was when I tried to answer questions. So writing and revising came easy.

"Well, Colonel Kane, we continue to bump into one another, in a manner of speaking."

"Wendy Eastland! We have to stop meeting like this. Your husband won't like it."

"I don't think he'll mind, Colonel. That's why I brought him along. Leiden, this is the notorious Killer Kane."

"Good to meet you, Mr. Secretary," I said, shaking his hand. "I fear you have me at a disadvantage. The swimming is obligatory like everything else at this base is obligatory, though I frustrate the system as best I can by exceeding the required number of lengths. And I'm only a lowly Captain."

Leiden Jeffries, a tall Gary Cooper kind of man with iron gray hair, was Assistant Undersecretary of Defense for Research and Evaluation. He and Gen. Rogers were a team at the Pentagon whose jobs were to prevent more of the same mistakes.

"My wife is always right, Colonel. You have been promoted to a lieutenant colonel. It is usually the custom to add in effect a double promotion along with the Medal of Honor."

Wendy and Leiden were an attractive couple in their middle thirties. They clearly liked me. Yet the contrarian in me—inherited from my old man—reared his head.

"I don't want no Medal of Honor."

They both gulped.

I leaned against the wall of the hospital.

"I don't like this war one bit. From beginning to end it has been phony, from 'shock and awe' to 'surge,' the Pentagon has deceived us and the American people. Not enough troops, no WMDs, inadequate armor, no response to roadside weapons, pathetic vehicles

like unarmored Jeeps and Humvees, idiots to administer an occu-
pation plan that didn't exist, insufficient Arab speakers, poor care
at VA and Army hospitals. This has been a snafued war from day
one—and that, Ms. Eastland, is all off the record."

They both looked frightened.

"He was much milder when he was a Captain," Wendy assured
her husband.

"Fred Rogers was sure you had strong opinions."

I relaxed and even smiled.

"They are stronger than the general realizes, sir. I will not begin
a campaign against the war while I'm on active duty. I have little to
add to the facts that are already on the record. And I will not go
over to the White House to add to their public-relations program
for the war."

"I doubt, Colonel, that our opinions on this subject differ mate-
rially from yours. We still have to get our troops out of country.
We need to establish criteria that might slow us down the next
time. Gen. Rogers and I are involved in a low key planning task
that we can surface after there is a change of administrations."

"The first thing we will need, sir, is a job description for a secretary of defense that a latter-day Don Rumsfeld won't fit."

Wendy Eastland intervened.

"We came here today to invite you to dinner in Landstuhl tonight, Pete, during which we can talk these matters over and you
don't have to stand in the corridor in your swimsuit and robe while
we argue."

"Fair enough," I said, finding my best Irish smile somewhere in
a deep pool of anger.

28

The restaurant in Landsthul was a typical German restaurant that had prospered from a half century of patronage from a major American base—thick oak walls, stiffly polite waiters, six-course dinners, and expensive red wine (of which I had one small glass) and a general feeling that this was the real Germany.

"Did you really go to heaven, Pete?" Wendy Eastland asked after our orders were taken.

"Deep background?"

"Everything we talk about tonight."

"There's a couple of shrinks over at the hospital who would like to send me off to a loony bin."

"I thought Dr. Irving cleared you." Leiden offered me a refill to my wine.

"No thanks—I'm still on meds and I don't want to give the shrinks an excuse to lock me up."

"I'll take care of them. Cindy is our very best. I've read the transcript. It was quite extraordinary, as much for the way you fended off Cindy as for your account."

"What was God like, Petey?"

"Delightful! You can let Wendy read it, so long as it's top secret until my book comes out."

"Deepest of deep background. What was Cindy's conclusion?"

"'Taking all the evidence into account there was nothing inconsistent with the possibility that there was an involvement with the transcendent'—or words to that effect."

"I assure you, Col. Kane, that the tape and the transcript are both completely confidential. Incidentally, I've brought them along for you."

He handed me a thick, sealed envelope.

"It is a most interesting document. One wants to believe it. As you say, any God who is not like the One is not worth believing in. . . . Look, I can finesse the Medal of Honor matter. Can we present it to you in, uh, Poplar Grove around Thanksgiving? We have read your master's paper and are impressed by your reflections on letters to home in the various wars. We will assign you to graduate studies on military issues at a university in your city to fulfill the rest of your obligations from your ROTC education. After that you might pursue any career you wish, though we would like you to stay in the reserve and perhaps act as a consultant to us in the future."

"I'd have to look over the fine print, but it sounds fine."

"Are you planning to go on the road to talk about heaven?"

"I'm not a priest, sir. But others can tell my story. I won't offend those evangelicals who won't believe in a laughing God."

"Here is my confidential card. It has my e-mail and phone numbers in case you need to get in touch with me."

"I won't lose this."

"They'll release you from here sometime in August. When do you expect your MA paper to be finished?"

"End of September. I'll work on it at West Point and then fly out to Texas A&M for my hearing. I hope to be home for Christmas."

"Sounds fine with me."

29

A week later Gen. Rogers found me in my room taking my afternoon nap, an indulgence to which I was becoming attached.

"Well, soldier, you seem to be recovering well."

"Very slowly, sir. The medics prescribe lots of food and lots of
sleep."

"As you were . . ."

"Thank you, sir."

But I popped out of bed and threw on my robe.

"You scared the daylights out of Mr. Jeffries."

"He said that he couldn't disagree with anything I said."

"He was surprised that a junior officer with ROTC background
could have developed such a detailed indictment of the war."

"I assume that I am not a junior officer anymore. I suspect, how-
ever, that most of the ROTC officers of my cohort would agree.
We're not really professional soldiers yet, sir. We won't be till the
West Pointers decide we're OK. And by then it's too late."

"Three Purple Hearts will generally do it for you. I'm also surprised that you refused to accept the Medal of Honor at the White House."

"If you wish, sir, I could reassess my decision."

"Certainly not, Peter. You are kind of a unique phenomenon; I'm inclined not to mess with you. I made that decision when you wanted to raid the house where our troopers were being prepared for the kill. Somehow I knew you'd carry it off."

"It was more than I knew, sir."

Gen. Rogers frowned, trying to figure me out. Forget it Freddy. Unique phenomenon, indeed.

I needed a wife to share such stories with.

After he left, I realized that I needed advice from my priest. I asked that I be connected with Fr. Joyce and gave them the number.

"Msgr. Joyce."

"Monsignor, Col. Kane is calling you from Ramstein Air Force Base in Germany. Will you speak to him?"

"I always speak to colonels. . . . Pete, what the hell has happened to the United States Army when they make you a colonel?"

"They have a lot of medals around that they need to get rid of before Congress begins to investigate. Besides, I'm only a lieutenant colonel."

"I'm glad to hear that."

"When are you coming over here?"

"I have reservations, Chicago to Frankfurt, for tomorrow night. AA Flight 1709."

"Oh."

"I figured you needed advice and you could hardly ask herself to fly to Ramstein to meet you."

"Gotta clean away the problems first. What would I need advice about?"

"Pete, it's pretty clear that you were dead and now you aren't dead anymore. I figure you might have paid a brief visit to the next world, and those in charge decided that they didn't want you. I wasn't consulted about this, which offends me. The least they could have done was ask for a letter from your parish priest."

Same old Jimmy. Actually it would have been nice to have Mariana along. Great fun. Maybe we could marry in the hospital chapel . . . No! I had to treat her with more respect.

"Should I tell the taxi driver to take me to the Ramstein-Landshtul Air Base and that I want to see Col. Kane?"

"Don't do that. The word hasn't got around here yet and the place is already crawling with my enemies. And, Fr. Jimmy, I have a list of books I would like you to bring . . ."

"I have purchased the usual reading list—Ring, Moody, Morse, Atwater, Bailey, Jansen, Blackmore, William James . . . In addition I have added Zaleski, which I had read already. She is the most sensible of the crowd."

"Thank you, I'm very grateful."

"You met Collette?"

"Yes. She is very happy. Keep that to yourself. I'm not sure how to handle that part of it yet. I'll ask the local chief chaplain to dispatch one of his assistants to meet you at the baggage carousal. He'll provide you housing for the night. He's not the swiftest priest in the world, but he's a real sweetheart."

"If I don't see you, I'll see you."

When I was in First Communion class, I thought all priests

were like Fr. Jimmy. It would be a lot better Church and world if they were.

I called the chief chaplain, himself a monsignor. He was besides himself with delight at the prospect of another purple-edged cleric.

There was a thought spinning wildly in my brain. What was it?

Call Mariana, you asshole! Now!

Right.

"Outgoing calls."

"In Chicago there is a lawyer named Mariana P. Pellegrino. Would you get her on the phone for me. Don't tell her who's calling."

In less than a minute, someone said brightly, "Mariana."

She pronounced her name with the appropriate Italian rolling-R sound. How much I missed that.

Then I lost all my courage. I wanted to run. I wanted to desert under fire. I wanted to disappear into the bowels of the earth.

"I've heard some interesting gossip, Mariana Pia. Peter Kane will be home for Christmas."

Silence that lasted forever.

A choked voice: "Petey, my darling, how wonderful!"

"Don't tell my mother. I'm going to call her next."

"You're really coming *home!*"

"Yep. I just spoke to Jimmy, so he would have all the red carpets cleaned and pressed. He's coming over, by the way. Bringing me books."

"This is not a dream, is it, Petey Pat?"

"No, not a dream . . ." so I was weeping too.

"You sound so wonderful. When will you be home?"

"They're giving me some kind of medal over at State U at their first-quarter commencement. Then I'll be on leave for a while and I'll enroll at the university to study for my doctorate."

I wanted desperately to spill out my life for her. But I must be careful. Don't push the poor woman. Give her time. It's time you learn how to be considerate.

Asshole! Coward! Ask her to come over with Jimmy and we can settle everything.

O you of little faith.

"You are really coming home! To stay!"

"I hope so."

"It will be so much better a neighborhood, Petey. Much better. I'm so happy!"

"There's a lot for us to talk about, Mariana."

"There's plenty of time to talk, Peter. Plenty of time."

"I'm going to call my mom now."

"Petey, she's so sweet to me. Be nice to her. Tell her that the old Petey is all gone."

"I'll try."

"Hi, Mom, it's Peter."

"Where are you, Peter?"

"In Germany. Ramstein Air Force Base. I've just learned my schedule for autumn. I expect to be home for Christmas."

"Isn't that nice, Peter. We'll all be glad to see you."

"The present plans are that I'll be in Chicago for some time. They're sending me back to school."

"Isn't that a good idea now?"

"Actually, I think it will be around Thanksgiving."

"We'll have a great big family dinner. Won't that be nice? I hope you called that poor girl?"

"Which poor girl?"

"The one who is too good for you altogether and yourself not knowing how lucky you are."

That was a dramatic change from her previous stance.

"I'm beginning to know," I said.

"Well, that's a good thing."

Mom was as happy at my good news as was Mariana. She had learned early in her life to dampen her emotions. But she had found a future daughter-in-law with whom she could connive, even without her son's presence. I could imagine them drowning the telephone lines in tears.

"You've grown up, Peter Patrick," Fr. Jimmy said as the young PFC put the box of books on the floor. "Thank you, Lenny."

He sat down on the extra chair in my quarters.

"You're welcome, Monsignor. You're staying tomorrow night too and you and Col. Kane will join the chaplains for supper?"

I nodded.

"We'll both be delighted."

"Thank you, Lenny," I said, "and my compliments to Col. Higgins."

"Yes, sir, Colonel, sir."

"You open the box," Jimmy said, "and I'll read your manuscript before I fall asleep." He glanced around my quarters. "Not much for a colonel."

"I'm not much of a colonel. Here's the manuscript and my illustrations."

"Michelangelo, don't look. This was from the inside."

All the books I needed were there. Naturally. I picked up *Other-world Journeys* by Carol Zaleski and began to read it.

"There's some personal things under the books."

I dug into the books and discovered two boxes of oatmeal-raisin cookies and a photograph of my once-and-future sweetheart in a modest (enough) strapless silver gown at a formal dance. No escort in sight. I gasped and then again. Even in the black-and-white photo, she sparkled.

"She is beautiful, Pete, and she needs you more than ever. They have not been easy years for her. The mother is on her all the time. She's a parent out of Jane Austen. Silvio can't protect her. Mariana moved out last year. She has a condo in the city and is very lonely. Her mother is one of the great bitches of the western world."

"All my fault."

"I forbid you to think that way, Peter Patrick Kane," he said as he sped through my manuscript. "Great picture of Collette. Heaven has been good for her. There is, I believe, another picture in the box."

"Have a raisin cookie."

"Thanks, I thought you would never ask."

"Marathon racer!"

Mariana in marathon garb, soaking wet, smiling happily.

A note was clipped to the second picture.

"Tomboy or superannuated deb. Which do you prefer? M. P."

"An athlete like you would prefer the racer, I suspect."

"More of her, anyway."

My imagination twisted in a spasm of desire. If I didn't think of a reason for not returning to Poplar Grove, I would become a permanent loser.

"This is all raw data?"

"I started to dictate it the day after I returned."

"The shrinks vet it?"

"The shrink in charge did. She added her own note at the end."

He went to the last page.

" 'Not inconsistent with a possible experience of the (T)transcendent!' Glory be to God! Peter Patrick Kane! This document is steeped in the transcendent!"

"I don't think I should show it to Mariana until after we're married."

"Very wise. It will shock her but it will also delight her. Even if her human lover can on the rare occasion be insensitive, the Lord of Creation adores her."

"He adores all of us, Jimmy."

"Patently, to use our new cardinal's favorite word. But she is extra special."

"I'm glad the God-person found it out. We've known it all along."

"That Jewish doctor-person was taken with you."

"Irish charm."

"With your family and your presumptive wife there cannot be too much of it."

He placed the papers back in the folder, straightened out the edges.

"I must reread this and think about it. And sleep on it . . . Speaking of sleep, you propose supper at some appropriate German restaurant?"

"I know of a nice place. Smells of sauerkraut."

"Regardless. Lenny will pick us up, he tells me. You will call the good Mariana and assure her that I arrived safely. She has been praying fervently for my safe journey all day."

I pushed Mariana's number at the office. Already I knew it by heart. Probably would never forget it.

"Mariana."

"The good monsignor arrived on time and is now resting his eyes at the base hotel."

"You opened the box?"

"I did. There were some delicious cookies and two pictures of a delicious woman."

"Which one did you like the most?"

"The runner, of course."

"I knew you'd say that!"

"I'll dream about both of them tonight."

"I hope you do."

31

As soon as we were seated at the restaurant, Jimmy removed the manuscript from the pocket of his suit coat.

"You did call your sweetheart. She continues to be ecstatic."

"I don't deserve that kind of adoration."

"No one does, but she has it to give and you must accept it gracefully. That's all you need to do to be a good husband to that poor young woman. You can forget about all confessions of guilt that are pent up in your melancholy, guilt-ridden Irish soul. Say 'I'm sorry' once and the past is forgotten."

"But I let her down!"

"You wrote this document. You think you would have been adequate for this woman when you were sixteen? Don't be ridiculous, Petey Pat!"

Jimmy was rarely so stern with anyone.

"When I was twenty-one?"

"No way. In fact, the current effort may still be a little premature."

His eyes twinkled. He was having me on.

"OK, I'll call her and tell her to chill out for five more years."

"Make sure your insurance policy is in good order before you do that. . . . Now to more serious matters. You wanted those books I couriered over because you are planning to write a book on your experiences in heaven?"

"I'm not sure . . ."

"But you're thinking about it. The matter is delicate, as they say in Rome. Therefore, I propose that you bookend it."

"Which means?"

"We have an intro by Cardinal Blackie and a postscript by Dr. Irving—the former to assure the world of your Catholic orthodoxy, and the latter of your sanity. They will both make the point that you're not pushing this story as true in every detail. It is an experience you had of God's goodness and love and wit when you were lingering between life and death, and such an experience is not inconsistent with the Catholic faith or mental health. Blackie will love it because he has always argued that God is, among other things, a comedian."

"You won't show him these notes and pictures, will you?"

"With your permission? He can fend off such heresy hunters as might invest their careers in your destruction. Once he reads this he will become quite difficult."

"Oh?"

"He will want it to be finished and published yesterday. That's the way he is."

"What about Mariana?"

"You don't show her this until after you are married, which will be soon."

"Hey, not so fast, Louie!"

"She will be shocked but pleased. Then she'll realize that you're writing a book and she will insist that she would tolerate no pseudonym. No sweat."

I wasn't so sure about that. What was the rush all about?

32

Television monitor. Col. Peter P. Kane is being interviewed by a hostile, very hostile journalist. Col. Kane is
wearing his dress blue uniform.

TV: How many deployments, Colonel?

PPK: Three, sir . . . well two and a half.

TV: Yes, let's see . . . (shuffles through papers). You were
    wounded in action. So you won a Purple Heart.

PPK: Yes, sir. It's easy. You just stand in the way of an en-
    emy bullet or ceremonial sword or suicide bomber.

TV: Has your unit been redeployed to . . .

PPK: Ft. Hood in Texas.

TV: Have you been cleared to return to Iraq?

PPK: No, sir.

TV (ACTING LIKE A PROSECUTING ATTORNEY): Why not?

PPK: They're watching me for PTSS.

TV: And what does that mean?

PPK: Post-traumatic stress syndrome.

TV: Isn't that a form of malingering?

PPK: I'm not a medical doctor, sir.

TV: You have three Purple Hearts?

PPK: Yes, sir, one with two clusters.

TV (AMAZED AND DISMAYED): It says here you will receive the Medal of Honor at State University after Thanksgiving.

PPK: Yes, sir.

TV: Why?

PPK: I don't know. I haven't read the citation.

TV (CAN'T FIND PAPERS HE IS LOOKING FOR): Can you tell us what happened in that battle that fortuitously excused you from fulfilling your deployment obligation?

PPK: As best as I can remember, sir. The last few moments are jumbled.

TV: Well, get on with the story.

PPK: A truck bomb exploded in front of a school in Baghdad, killing over a hundred children. My troop was deployed immediately to establish a perimeter to deal with a possible second bomb while the square in front of the school was filled with dead and wounded children, teachers, parents, and many American and Iraqi troops. The terrorists like these kind of attacks. Upon arrival, I established four roadblocks and manned them with my troops. I assumed command where I thought it most likely that the second bomber would attack—at a T-shaped intersection, perhaps seventy-five yards from the center of the square. I observed a cab speeding down the street toward us. I instructed my squad to fire over the cab's roof. It did not slow down. I have seen such vehicles before and my instincts told me that it was the second bomber. I ordered my soldiers to take cover, and advanced around the ruined Fiat that was our barrier and delivered

automatic-weapon fire into the motor block of the
vehicle. It stopped immediately and blew up. Then
a much bigger and probably secondary explosion occurred. I was thrown into the air and over the car. I am
told I landed on my head. I was medivaced to the field
hospital where I was judged dead on arrival. The monitor reported no brain waves.

TV: But you're still alive?

PPK: I think so, sir.

TV: What happened?

PPK: I'm told that after nine and a half minutes, my brain
began to function again. I later learned that similar incidents were in the literature about suicide bombing.
A few long interludes before revival have in fact been
longer than mine. No record . . . You can understand
why the army wants to keep an eye on me before they
send me back to Iraq. Candidly, I'm inclined to leave
that choice to the medics.

TV: A remarkable story, Colonel. Was it recorded on tape?

PPK: I'm told it was, sir, but I have not asked to see it. My
father, who is a first-generation Irish American, says
that it was a good thing I had inherited his hard head.

TV: Remarkable. Now, a committee of the Senate has just returned from Iraq. They report that the GIs are hoping that the government does not end the war before victory. Their morale, the senators say, is sky-high. Can you confirm that situation?

PPK: I have been out of country for several months, sir. I don't doubt that some soldiers said that to the senators. However, it was not the kind of comment that was routine in my outfit. In all the wars our country has fought except the Civil War, soldiers want to stay alive, defeat the enemy, protect their buddies, finish the job, and return home. They would cheer if the war was suddenly over. In the Civil War men on both sides believed in the reasons given by their leaders. Six percent of the adult men in the country died— a loss that would haunt America for the rest of the century.

TV (FURIOUS BECAUSE HE CANNOT FIND THE PAPERS FOR WHICH HE WAS LOOKING): Col. Kane, you are a coward and perhaps a traitor. You clearly support those who want to surrender in Iraq. You are unworthy to wear the Medal of Honor.

(TRIES TO WRAP UP THE INTERVIEW)

PPK: Just a moment, sir. Don't you dare cut me off. I don't think I'm worthy of the Medal either. As for cowardice

I point to my three Purple Hearts. And as for surrender, as long as I'm an officer on active duty, I will not express a personal opinion regarding strategy on the public record. I am entitled to my private opinion about whether withdrawing from a war that was unwisely entered is surrender.

33

Monitor again. PPK is present on the camera. Interviewer is Wendy Eastland.

EASTLAND: Can I begin, Col. Kane, by asking how you are feeling. I was there when you were thrown over the car and thought that your career was finished.

PPK: I'm fine, Wendy. Relieved to be going home for the first time since I was commissioned.

EASTLAND: The doctors have cleared you for active duty?

PPK: Yes and no, Wendy. I've been cleared for active duty with the caveat that reassignment to combat should be delayed for a year or two. So they're sending me to the university to study the importance of morale to soldiers in war time.

EASTLAND: How do you feel about not returning to Iraq?

PPK: I am happy that I won't have to go back at once. Otherwise I will obey the decisions of my commanding officers.

EASTLAND: Might I say that you are a good deal more mature than when I first interviewed you in Iraq.

PPK: Combat command has a way of maturing a person, Wendy.

EASTLAND: Why will you be receiving the medal at State U instead of the White House?

PPK: It's the anniversary of the first graduation class of militia at State U. The leadership of the university wants to make something out of it.

EASTLAND: If you had been ordered to go to the White House for the award, would you have gone?

PPK: I did not have to make that decision. I would have simply declined the medal. I had no desire to be part of a public relations event.

EASTLAND: What will you do now?

PPK: Give some serious thought to growing up. The PP, you know, stands for Peter Pan.

EASTLAND: Do you think you will marry?

PPK: Women are a lot more attractive than when I left Poplar Park. I'm told that married men have to mature in a hurry.

EASTLAND: What is the most important attribute you would seek in a woman you might marry?

PPK: Patience. And lots of it.

EASTLAND: Pete, were you really dead in the hospital that evening?

PPK: My brain waves were flat for nine and a half minutes, more if you add the time required to bring me to the field hospital. I was pronounced clinically dead.

EASTLAND: Then what?

PPK: Then I was in heaven.

EASTLAND: Really?

PPK: Really! I talked to God; argued with God, in fact.

EASTLAND: Did you win the argument?

PPK: No one wins an argument with God. The surprise is that God loves to argue. Loves to laugh, too.

EASTLAND: That's hardly a Christian teaching, is it, Pete?

PPK: St. Therese, the Little Flower, once said that God is nothing but mercy and love. That was the God I encountered in heaven. I think that's the Father in heaven that Jesus came to talk about. I know that everything will be all right and that there's nothing to worry about.

EASTLAND: You wanted to stay there.

PPK: Sure I did. Who wouldn't? But God wanted me to go back to do something very important. No one that encounters God's love could ever refuse a request. I tried. You can't fight the Lord thy God.

EASTLAND: Did the army psychiatrists think you were mad?

PPK: The psychiatrist in charge of me said that I had an ecstatic experience of the peace and joy not inconsistent with an experience of the transcendent. She said that the word might be spelled with a capital T.

EASTLAND: All of this will be in a book you are writing that will be out next summer. What will it be called?

PPK: *To Heaven and Back.*

EASTLAND: Do you remember the last words in your argument with God?

PPK: I said to him something like "I guess we are all chained by the bonds of love." And then God laughed his rich wonderful laugh and said, "Tell me about it."

EASTLAND: God speaks the language of an American adolescent?

PPK: God can speak all languages because he invented us to speak languages. So he talks the language of the one to whom he is speaking. I guess he thinks I'm an American adolescent, just a bit superannuated.

34

"Kane."

"Petey, you were wonderful this morning!"

"Who is this calling?"

"Mariana . . ."

"Where is my weapon?"

"Weapon!"

"I can't find it!"

"Pete, what's wrong?"

"How did you get my number?"

"Jimmy gave it to me!"

"This is a secure line. Please end this message."

"Where are you, Petey?"

"I'm in the ready room! You must have the wrong number!"

"*Pete darling!* You're at West Point!"

"Have I been transferred . . . What am I doing at West Point?"

"Doing research!"

"I am not assigned to research."

"No, Pete, my love, you're having bad dreams. You have been re-deployed."

"Dreams . . . I'm at West Point?"

"Don't you remember? You were on national television this morning, talking about your journey to heaven."

"Heaven . . . who is this again?"

"Mariana . . ."

"Mariana Pia Elizabeta Angelina Pellegrino?"

"I woke you up in the middle of a nightmare."

"Nightmare . . . I'm sorry. They don't happen very often. I must have been in a deep, deep sleep."

"I'm sorry I woke you up."

"I'm not . . . It's nice to wake up to your voice . . . I should do it more often. Would you please wake me up from every nightmare for the rest of my life?"

"Now you're my sweet, darling Petey Pat from first grade, full of fun and laughter!"

"And full of images of you in a thin nightgown."

"Peter! I'm not in bed! It's only six P.M. here in Chicago!"

"Worse luck for my dirty thoughts."

"I called to tell you my dad and I went over to your house today with Msgr. Jimmy to watch the TV . . ."

"First time you didn't see a program on the big screen!"

"And your family was very nice. Your dad has a great sense of humor. He's been on the wagon for years now . . ."

"Since the time I floored him."

"You gotta forgive, Petey Pat."

"Don't we all."

"You were your old self. Neither interviewer was ready for you."

"I think Wendy was mostly ready. Your mom didn't come, did she?"

"She denies she watched it at home, but she's lying like she usually does. Well, anyway, I don't want to keep you. Pleasant dreams."

"I'll have wonderful erotic dreams about you."

"Don't you dare."

It was almost as though the Lord my God was whispering in my ear.

You're running out of time. She loves you as much as she ever did. You either claim her now or you lose her permanently. She's waited a long time for you. If you don't ask her to marry you before you head to the university, she'll figure that you're not interested.

I'm not sure that I am.

You mean that you're still scared of her.

There's no point in arguing with You.

None at all.

I need more time. So does she.

You're not going to have more time. You let this chance slip away and you've lost her. We will all have lost her.

I won't lose her.

You know you have competition.

Who?

You know about this doctor her mother is pushing—Wainwright Burke.

I'm not afraid of him.

Maybe you should be.

This was not necessarily the One whispering in my ear.

However, I'm sure he was thinking the same thing. I could be in real trouble if I didn't shape up.

I consoled myself as I fell back to sleep with images of her in bed in a thin nightgown with me beside her.

The next morning the voice whispered in my ear again, "Why don't you draw that picture?"

"What picture?"

"The one of her in the thin nightgown."

"You want me to seduce myself?"

No answer.

35

Commencement day at State U was a wet, dreary day. My Thanks-giving reunion with my family had been a huge success. My father has been in AA for five years, he told me, and it was the best thing he ever did besides marrying my mother. He drove a FedEx deliv-ery truck, which didn't pay as much as the long haul but was not nearly as hard on the nerves. His kinky black hair had turned white and he looked and acted like a mellow leprechaun. I don't care about this war, he whispered to me, but we're damn proud of you. The army didn't start the war, I replied.

Mom was slim and trim and proud of her job as a sales manager at a computer service firm over in the Poplar shopping mall. My younger siblings, all teens, two boys and two girls, seemed good-natured and healthy. Paul had been offered a scholarship as a pitcher at St. Ben's. "Get it in writing," I had warned him.

No one said anything about my trip to heaven and back, but they had high praise for "Monsignor"—the best priest I've ever known according to mom. The girl siblings told me that Mariana was like totally cool. "She's waited all these years for you, Pete! That's, you know, ecstatic."

"Don't let her get away," my dad warned me.

Five years and two punches had created that drastic a change! I'd better find someone else to punch.

Mariana? No way.

At my mother's suggestion I had reserved a small room for myself at the Poplar House, a rehabbed Edwardian hotel, right across from the park. Its single bed precluded the possibility of it becoming a love nest. To propose to Mariana terrified me. I would die of shame if I dared proposition her. I also reserved a room for Gen. Rogers and his wife, who would fly out the night before the ceremony. Wendy and Secretary Jeffries would fly in to State Park on a helicopter. WTN would have a TV crew set up at State U. I asked that my parents, Mariana, and her parents be invited to the luncheon and that seats in the small auditorium be reserved for Marty Finn, Tommy O'Brien, Jane Quinlan, Reen Connors, and their respective spouses. Presumably the One would provide facilities for Collette and Joey.

I had prepared some stupid remarks and promptly forgot them when I awoke in the morning. To hell with it. You either had the gift of gab or you didn't.

Nancy and Fred Rogers were prepared to calm me down at the breakfast table in Poplar House. They seemed quite surprised that I was my usual casual self.

"My friends at the Pentagon were impressed by your performance on TV," the general said, with some surprise. "They have paid you the high compliment that you are 'unique.'"

"May they continue to think that."

"They also want to see your new book as soon as it is published."

"I will personally autograph as many as you ask, sir."

"You don't seem at all uneasy, Peter," Nancy Rogers said.

"What's to be afraid of? Not you or the general, not the local brass. I kissed the blarney stone. That's enough."

"Will the young woman be there?" Gen. Rogers asked.

"What young woman?"

I knew, of course. Fred Rogers had read Cindy's paper.

"The one you're going to marry."

"How wonderful!"

Mrs. Rogers, mother of two daughters, was always delighted to hear that some young men were abandoning their freedom. Freedom was not my problem. Or was it?

"Mariana," her husband reminded me.

"Well, to keep my parents happy we invited her and her parents. They'll be at lunch and I suppose at the ceremony. I haven't had time to see her since I've been back. I'm afraid of her. If she frowns at me I might panic."

"Fat chance," the general said. "Wendy Eastland is dying to meet her."

"I'm told that Mariana hates Wendy. They'll have to introduce themselves. They'll bond immediately and join forces against me."

"You've slept with her?" Nancy Rogers asked.

"I wouldn't dare try."

I was easing into my Petey Pat leprechaun modality.

We formed up at the HQ building of the ROTC unit, even more tattered and wormy than it had been when I attended my

MS (Military Science) classes there—courses taught mostly by officers who had failed at everything else. Yet when wars started, the "citizen soldiers" had been indispensable. They deserved, I had always thought, better preparation than we received. Yet both our guys and the West Pointers were equally inept at first, though they were both presumably career officers while we were destined to be called up to fill in the slots. In combat, I had observed—perhaps with some prejudice—that our asshole rate was no lower than theirs. Nobody was any good the first time under fire.

The rain stopped and with lots of rituals and slapping of weapons we formed up and marched over to the auditorium, Gen. Rogers and me in our dress blues, looking like maybe we planned on marching to Vicksburg the next morning.

There was a considerable ritual of presenting colors and saluting and such stuff that I barely remembered. As the party destined for the platform passed the front row of honored guests, I noted that Mariana was sitting next to Wendy. Already thick as thieves.

I leaned over and touched Mariana's lips.

"Good to see you again," I whispered.

"Petey," she said, breathless and flushed.

The corps cheered enthusiastically.

The president of State University introduced Gen. Rogers at great length.

The general mounted the podium.

"I was CO of Col. Kane's division in Iraq. Commanders of other units said that he would ruin my career eventually if I didn't calm him down. In particular I ordered the action, mentioned in the citation, in which he rescued some of our men and women from execution by terrorists. He called me on the phone to tell me what he intended to do to rescue them. I replied that I didn't want to know what he was going to do, he should just do it. That shows the confidence I had in his intelligence, leadership, and bravery. He brought them all back alive and he was the only casualty, a sword slash in his side. I am proud to read this citation and proud to have been with him in Iraq."

I had read the citation that morning and told the general I thought it was excessive. He pinned the blue and white ribbon on my uniform and we saluted sharply. I caught Mariana's eye and grinned.

"I am grateful to Gen. Rogers for traveling to the prairie soil of this state to pin this ribbon on my dress blues, which leads some people in this part of our country to think that I work for the United States Coast Guard, our oldest service, and one to whose membership I am not worthy. 'Always ready,' they say. There were a lot of times when we were not ready.

"I remember standing in this auditorium, knowing that I was destined for the desert, and experiencing the emotion which is generally called 'scared stiff.' You put a man or a woman through some courses, send them to summer camp, give him a new uniform with a gold bar on his shoulder and tell him he's now a leader, responsible for the lives of his subordinates and civilians and, necessarily, leave him on his own. They told us here in this auditorium that we were the essential leaders of our military. I didn't think we could possibly do it. Turns out that we could. We were the officer corps of this Republic. We were the heirs of the militia at Valley Forge; the jungle fighters of the Philippines; the new recruits in the Hürtgen Forest; the Battered Bastards of Bastogne, as the 101st Airborne called themselves; X Corps, who landed at Inchon; the men who entered Iraq without proper armor or adequate vehicles, or any clear sense of what we were supposed to do. We survived, most of us, and slipped back into the obscurity of civilian life with a link to the reserve because it was still our army. In some countries such an officer corps would be laughed at. Yet in a country like this one, our officer corps must be part civilian if we are not to become an oversized Prussia.

"The events described in the citation may have in sum required no more than five minutes. My actions as a CO were instinctive, unplanned, inexcusably lucky. I prayed a lot. I even asked TV interviewers to pray for me. All I can recommend to you, my young friends, is that you pray too and trust in your instincts and never forget your obligation to protect the lives of those under you. God bless you all."

The audience responded with a standing ovation. I saluted Gen. Rogers briskly and walked with parade ground precision back to my chair. My First Communion mates in the front row were the first to their feet and my adorable Mariana beat the rest of them. Not bad for a hastily planned ad lib.

On the way out, I hugged Mom and Wendy Eastland and kissed Mariana more decisively than the first time. Walking down the aisle I became aware that my legs had turned to water.

"Nothing ever scares you, Pete," Gen. Rogers remarked at the lunch table later on.

"A suicide bomber in a taxi scares me, General, sir."

No one was wise enough to assign Mariana and myself to the same table. I told myself that, well, I could hardly propose to her in such circumstances.

However, she took the initiative.

"Col. Kane, sir, I have two invitations. I'm having a small buffet dinner party at my condo next Saturday to celebrate your safe return to Poplar Grove. Jane and Marty will drive you down. I'll promise to be well behaved. I know how busy you are reacclimating to America, but if you could squeeze it in . . ."

"I'm sure I can, Ms. Pellegrino, ma'am."

"Now I'll push my luck. The Christmas dance at the club? It's formal, as you know. So maybe . . ."

"You have a mildly scandalous gown in red or green?"

"Red."

"I'll look forward to holding you in my arms for the whole evening. And I'll wear my blue formals. We'll make quite a colorful couple."

If I can find a place to buy them, I thought.

She smiled. "We'll be all of that. Since it's at the club, I'll pick you up in my most recent Jaguar. You will drive, of course."

"Of course."

"Your mom?" I asked.

"We hardly speak to each other. It's hard on my dad. He still loves her."

36

The party at her condo in the city was a disaster.

Marty, Jane, and I arrived promptly at eight o'clock. Two young men were already there—handsome, intense, self-confident, with short hair, one blond, one brown. They were beyond doubt young physicians, so young that because they knew a lot about one or two important things they were serenely confident that they knew everything about everything. The blond, so gracefully pretty that my hostile mind labeled him gay, introduced himself as Dr. Burke and his buddy as Dr. Gross. Mariana wasn't on the scene.

"Pete," I said.

"Col. Pete, isn't it?"

"I'm not on duty."

"What's the medical care over there like?" Dr. Gross asked as he put a glass of Coca-Cola in my hand. It tasted of rum—or what I imagined rum would taste like.

"No thanks," I said. "I don't drink. The medical care in country is very good, mostly top-flight people who were in the reserves. The same is true of the hospital at Ramstein in Germany. Back in this country it leaves much to be desired."

"You don't drink because you're one of those PTSD people?" Dr. Burke asked. "The kind that go postal and kill everyone in the room."

"I didn't have a concussion, so that's probably not likely. But my shrink told me to stay away from the creature for a year or so."

"You don't want a taste of this wonderful martini? Best this side of Harvard."

Marty and Jane declined. Dr. Burke shrugged, poured a martini glass and slugged down the contents in a single swallow.

The guy was a jerk. How could Mariana have become involved with him and then invite him to this party? I didn't want a contest with a rival, especially if he were drunk.

Mariana herself arrived with a platter of exquisite appetizers. She was wearing a wide flowing gown and her golden hair was bound up over her head.

"Pete has never drank," she said firmly.

She gave me a bottle of Lipton's green iced tea.

"The big military hero drinks Lipton's green tea," Dr. Burke sniggered. "John Wayne would never do that."

"I never served in his outfit," I said.

The condo was not one of those skyscrapers along the lake. Rather it was a comfortable converted six flat, a couple of blocks from the lake. She had decorated it like it was in Milan or Florence or maybe Venice—places I knew only by reputation and the occasional travel brochure.

"Florence?" I asked her.

"Close enough."

She kissed my cheek, a hasty peck.

Uh-oh, I was in trouble too . . . that wasn't fair.

Three women entered the parlor with large carts; two others appeared with TV tables. We were instructed to eat as much as we wanted. There were, after all, two doctors present to take care of us. My beloved was angry. I would try to avoid that anger.

Sniggers from Drs. Burke and Gross. Burke was busy mixing another martini container.

"Hey, you don't really believe that near-death shit, do you, Colonel, sir? It's a lot of rubbish, you know. Takes in a lot of the evangelicals, you know. But it's all phony. When you're dead, you're dead!"

"Well, I was dead for nine and a half minutes."

"And you went to heaven and talked to God."

"I had a transcendental experience, is how my doctors described it."

"Yeah, and it changed your life, I suppose."

"Not enough time to be sure," I said, my voice tense.

Marty Finn eased over next to me. There was not going to be a fight. I would walk out on the party before I floored the SOB.

"Look, Colonel, I'm a doctor, you know. That means I'm a scientist, you know. Scientists, you know, don't believe in that bunkum. When you're dead, you're dead. It's all over. Finished. Done."

"You've reviewed literature on the subject and reached that as a balanced conclusion?"

"At Harvard, we don't review literature on shit."

I put two ribs drenched with sauce on a plate and tried to figure out how to eat them. Jane whispered to me, "Fingers."

She thereupon left for the kitchen to fetch the boss lady.

"There are scientists," Wainwright Burke continued, "who have duplicated the same phenomenon by injecting chemicals into the brain. It's just a way of sedating someone who is dying. Just brain chemicals."

He was growing woozy and ready to fight. I'd never been in a bar fight in all my life. I didn't want to go to the mat with this guy, not in this elegant apartment with the fawn-colored carpets—on which the good doctor had just spilled half a glass of martini.

"Do you know a journal called *The Lancet*?"

"Sure I know it. British journal. First-rate. You gotta at least look at the titles of the articles to keep up with things."

"There is an article in an issue of it by four Dutch physicians who did research on men who had died with a stroke and then revived. They concluded there was no evidence of brain-chemical activity during the flat time. None."

Mariana had appeared with a sponge, a rag and a spray gun in her hand. She knelt on the floor to clean the martini spill. Dr. Gross removed the mixer from his friend's hand.

"I don't give a fucking damn about fucking Dutch physicians," Burke continued. "It's all hokum. And you might get more promotions by pushing that bullshit and appealing to the fundamentalists, but you're just a fraud and a faker and a mountebank."

I'd give it one more try.

"I'm not convinced that the experience proves anything. I never try to change anyone's mind. I just say that I have made up my own mind that the NDE experience is a hint. I've always liked hints."

"Well, I'll give you a hint: you've got your blue suit and your fancy medal, but you're nothing but a fucking mountebank."

"Marty?" I said.

"Right away."

I kissed Mariana's forehead.

"I think I'd better leave now, Mariana."

She nodded her head in agreement.

We left.

"What was that all about?" I asked as our SUV eased out of the small parking place in front of the apartment building.

"Two male apes fighting over an attractive female ape," Jane snapped.

"Yeah, but why did Mariana invite him?"

"I don't know. She's strange about him. It's all her mother's idea. He's a nice young man and he comes from a wonderful family and has a great career ahead of him."

"He's halfway to alcoholism."

"Three-quarters," Marty agreed. "Poor Mariana wants a family. At twenty-five she figures she's an old maid. Her mother keeps telling her that. Why mess with a dubious warrior off in the desert when such a nice young man loves you?"

"Does he?"

Jane sighed.

"I'm not sure. But why set up a battle with you that he couldn't possibly win?"

"Because he's still there and I'm not?"

37

Poplar Grove is an old suburb. Construction came to an end before the beginning of World War II. Most of the homes are large with big yards. Those at the south end are older, many of them wood construction, some even dating to the Civil War. It began as a rural escape for the city's most successful businessmen who could ride in twenty minutes from their offices downtown to the Poplar Station. Later a rapid-transit system provided a second line that went into the north end of town. The transportation convenience kept home values in the town high. It did not turn into a suburban slum like its neighbors. Originally it was solidly Protestant; now it is solidly Catholic. St. Regis (St. John Francis Regis to give the proper name) is the mother Church on the east side of town. Its wooden church was built in 1860 and covered with white stone in 1930, ruining its original beauty. The school is big and modern because one of the pastors had sense enough to know that a quality school would sustain loyalty no matter how crazy the next pastor might be. Since the parish's east–west boundaries crisscross the North End and the South End, our little house next to the railroad tracks and the Pellegrino palace in the North End are in the same parish. So Mariana and I were in the same class for seven years. Poor radiant little Mariana, so lively, so curious, so much fun—ruined by that terrible mother of hers. I had let her down.

Poplar Mall, a half mile north of the town limits—a vast collection of capitalistic temples with few poplar trees save those marking the lanes for parking—was a convenience that we used when necessary, but whose existence we deplored. But Poplar Street was a small business district near the railroad tracks, with corner stores, an ice cream fountain, a cookie store, boutique shops, intellectual highbrow emporia, and arts-and-craft things, combined with meat markets and bakeries and laundromats.

The poplar trees that gave the area its name flourished. There are more now than there were a hundred and fifty years ago. Everyone wants a tree in their front lawn or their backyard. Lots of leaves to rake up in autumn, but glorious green lace in spring. I had taken it for granted as a kid.

I left hating it. Now I was rediscovering it at Christmas time, perhaps its best season. Msgr. Jimmy had found the rolls that played the chimes in the new bell tower of the church. So Christmas carols rang out often on the crisp winter air and snowflakes covered the nakedness of lawns and trees. Elaborate Christmas displays—not always tasteful—shone through the trees, turning the whole town to a kind of magic park. And the park itself, the pride of the city, came alive with snowmen and sleds and skis and skaters. I had been away for seven years and now, pilgrim of the many-colored lands, had come home and recognized it for the first time.

And poor Mariana, hesitant and shy at first, had spent her childhood years in Rome and was afraid that no one in this new hometown of hers would like her and want to know her. Instead all of us fell in love with her. And I had let her down. I had left her for too long. Our group never really survived after Joey and Collette had died and I left town.

So I am angry at her for the farce at her condo. But still she had invited me twice to provide an occasion for reconciliation—since I was incapable of taking the first step.

Tonight could be my last chance.

38

Her father opened the door.

"I am superstitious, Peter," he said, "but I'm sure the mother of Jesus will protect the two of you on this glorious night."

"I still don't drink, sir."

"I was very proud of you when you spoke at State University. I said to some of the young men with whom I talked later that you were my daughter's boyfriend."

"Is that what I am, sir, after all these years?"

"She has never claimed another."

Then she walked down the stairs, a vision that turned off the glow in my memory of prom night. Back then she was a budding woman, uneasy in her new role. Now she was a poised, self-possessed woman of the world who was entitled to an escort of a thousand admirers instead of a brat kid she had met in first grade. Her gown was a brilliant Christmas red, strapless but protected by a matching red scarf. The dress did not quite reach her knees so there could be no doubt about her long and shapely athletic legs. Mariana Pia was well covered, only not covered at all. She stopped halfway down the steps, dazzled by my glittering blue formals and my chest of medals. And I gaped at her beauty, as if I had seen it only for the first time.

"I'll bring her home safely tonight, sir," I said as I draped a white cloak around her shoulders. "This time I promise."

We all laughed. Uneasily.

Then I realized, maybe for the first time since my visit to the city, that the Lord my God wanted me to protect Mariana. From what?

From an early death? This was not only a choice I could make. It was part of the One's scenario. I had to save her, tonight, or it could be never.

"I'm sorry about the other night," she said as I opened the car door for her. "I thought you would assume that I didn't invite that asshole."

"Forgive me for assuming till this minute that you did."

"That's understandable, I suppose. It was my mother who told him about the party so he could come and intimidate you and ruin my celebration. I should have ordered him out, but he wouldn't have left. I was angry at you for leaving. You could have creamed him. Then I realized you didn't want to have a public fight with him . . ."

"It is such a nice apartment," I said, resisting the impulse to take my arm off the wheel and put it around her. "I didn't want to spoil the furniture."

"If he had so much as touched you, I would have gone after him with my claws."

"Finally he left?"

"Shortly after you did. Jane called me the next morning and said I'd blown it."

"I had to come tonight because I wanted to see what your Christmas wrapping paper was like."

"You weren't mad at me, Pete?"

"I was baffled. And besides, I was acting childishly and thought I'd better get out of there quickly before I did something really stupid."

Our entry onto the dance floor created a sensation.

"Where did you find the redhead, Mar?" a sharp-looking matron asked as we walked by her.

"Down at the shops. He was second prize."

"The first?"

"A ticket to the Bulls game last night."

"Congratulations on the award, Colonel. Did you know that Harry Truman used to say that he would rather be able to wear that medal than be president?"

"We already have one candidate from this state."

"How bad is it over there, Pete?"

"Not as bad as Omaha Beach or Iwo Jima or Fredericksburg . . ."

"You're really good at this stuff, Col. Pete," she said, her eyes glowing with approval.

"Petey Pat always had the last word."

"I remember. He was just a loudmouth punk."

"I don't deny it."

"With a funny blue ribbon on his Coast Guard uniform."

"I don't dance this well," I protested.

"Don't worry, I'll guide you and they will all marvel."

"They won't forget I was a klutz."

"You *never* were a klutz! Only a little geeky sometimes."

As the night and the dinner and the dancing and the singing went on, the two of us unaccountably became tense, edgy, snappish. Why should we be snappish? We loved each other, didn't we? We had waited for years to overcome the traumas of prom night and my cowardice. Everyone knew our story and they were watching us to see what would happen. The result at that age in our lives was enormous sexual tension. Would we spend the rest of our lives together, in the same house, in the same bedroom, with the same children? Had we not both changed tremendously? We were no longer two kids in the school yard of St. Reg's with a prepuberty crush on each other, were we? If we were to join our lives and bodies did we not need time to get to know each other? But we didn't have that time. Our friends, our families, our neighborhood wanted a happy ending. Was it not a question of now or never? And wasn't never a much wiser and more prudent choice? Was not a marriage now an invitation to disaster?

Maybe we should go over to St. Reg's and consult with Msgr. Jimmy?

I knew what he would say. OK, but he wouldn't have to live through the anxieties, the adjustments, the emotional extremes of postmarital letdowns and fights. Tonight was the time to speak honestly to each other and end this foolish prom-night love affair revival. Wasn't I displaying a studied maturity that would save us from a disastrous mistake we would regret for the rest of our lives?

What about my friend the Lord thy God?

Did I still believe the basic theme of that encounter with the transcendent—that from eternity, this delicious bundle of womanliness in my arms and I had been designed for each other?

I wasn't sure.

So I left it to her to take the initiative.

"Peter, I would like to talk seriously for a few minutes."

Yep. She would be able to commend herself for the rest of her life on superior wisdom. She had climbed the moral high ground and seen our future and found it in ruins.

"Sure."

"There's a supplementary coatroom that faces out on the eighth hole . . . I know how to lock the door."

"Will I be safe?"

Dumb thing to say.

"I don't think that's the issue."

Somewhere in the background I thought I heard laughter— the Deus Jocoso laughing at our folly.

You keep out of this, I told him.

But he continued to laugh.

Inside our little retreat, the snow-covered eighth fairway spread out in front of us, shining in the light of the quarter moon and providing a chill background for delectable Mariana Pia to deliver her opening statement of the case.

"This isn't going to work, is it, Pete? It's not your fault, it's not my fault. It is what it is. We've been on separate paths for too long—seven years. We've tried to keep alive the dreams of our early school days at St. Reg's. Maybe we could have gone down the same path together when we were seventeen. We can't now. What happened at the condo was understandable. My mom won. But we didn't call each other. We both hoped it might all go away. We've been tense all evening. We're both scared and we want it to end. Tonight is the time to do it before it becomes even more difficult and we hurt each other more than we already have. I will always have a warm place in my heart for you, Petey Pat, but we both know it wouldn't work."

She prepared wonderful briefs for her law firm.

She kissed my cheek and turned toward the door of our closet. She flipped off the lock and walked through the door.

"Mariana," I barked in my best parade-ground voice, "don't you ever turn your back on me again!"

She stopped in her tracks. Her muscles and bones seemed to melt. Her firm, shapely back caved in. She slumped like she was about to collapse on the floor. She turned toward me again, her head bowed, her shoulders sagging, her breasts dejected.

"What's more, don't ever try to walk away on me again! And that's an order."

"Peter, how can I walk away from you? You are my salvation!"

We stumbled into each other's arms.

I would have to find out later what "salvation" meant.

I held her fiercely.

"You're mine, woman, and don't you ever try to get away from me again." I caressed her gently and kissed her with infinite tenderness. It was just the two of us together. We could cope with anything.

"I don't want to be anything else."

We would have to nuance a lot, negotiate the bumps in the road, redeploy the dragons and demons inside both of us. But we could do that. I had wooed her and won her and would bed her soon.

You hear that, the Lord my God?

He was out there on the golf course laughing at us.

"You are very good at this sort of thing, Petey Pat," she said with a sigh.

"What sort of thing?"

"Remote foreplay."

"Is that what it is?"

"Hmm . . ."

The Jocose Deity faded away, though his laughter trailed behind him.

"You know what we must look like?" I asked.

"Hungry lovers?"

"Hungry lovers don't sob in each other's arms."

"Are we both sobbing? I guess we are."

"We're two survivors. A hurricane or a tornado or flash flood swept us away. But we survived. And we are pledging that we will continue to survive. With the help of God we will make it."

"Whatever."

The same waves of love washed over me that bathed me in the City.

"Shall we marry?"

It had just slipped out. I hadn't prepared it anymore than my talk at State Park. The die had been cast.

Gotcha.

So the Lord my God had not left us.

"Oh yes, Peter love! Yes! Yes! Yes! And soon!"

"When?"

"Christmas Eve! That way I won't have to buy you a present. I'll be your Christmas gift."

"And you're already wearing your wrapping paper."

"Let's go over to the rectory and tell Msgr. Jimmy."

39

Msgr. Jimmy opened the door. He was wearing his usual uniform of black jeans and black sweatshirt, and holding a book in his hand. He probably had fallen asleep over the book at the end of his day.

"We want to marry," Mariana announced brightly.

"On Christmas Eve after the 6:30 morning Mass."

"And get it over with."

He blinked a couple of times.

"Why am I not surprised? Come in! It's cold outside."

"We don't notice it, Jimmy."

"Well, congratulations! It's time enough, I guess. I admire your courage. I thought you'd mess around with it. Good! Get it done."

"Don't we get a lecture about thinking it over carefully?" Mariana sounded disappointed.

"I don't think the two of you are in any condition to think *anything* over."

True enough.

"You'll need a marriage license and a dispensation from the bans. You get the former. I'll get the latter."

"We'll go downtown for the license tomorrow," she said. "My mom and dad can't stop us, can they?"

"I have some clout down there, you might remember. I propose that I call Marty and Jane and tell them to show up in the Church at 6:15 and keep any suspicions a secret. Those two will. Then you retreat to your bower in the woods . . ."

"Marriage suite at Poplar House."

"And reappear, radiantly happy, for the midnight Mass. The very angels in heaven will celebrate simultaneously the rebirth of hope in the birth of Jesus and in the rebirth of your love."

The marriage license was no problem. She deputed me to go to her favorite jeweler to purchase Claddagh wedding rings while she selected her wedding dress.

I also bought her a very large diamond. We would work out our financial protocols later and I would tell her about the advance on my book. She had the good taste not to question the cost of the ring, though she almost did. The next morning she picked me up at Poplar House in her Jaguar and drove me over to the Church. She wore a coat so I could not see her wedding dress until we were in the sacristy before Mass. Jane approved enthusiastically. Marty and I just stared.

"A suggestion, Mr. and Mrs. Kane," Jimmy said. "There will be a dustup with your parents after Mass. Don Silvio will simmer down and concede that it was your marriage. You two should be prepared for Petey to say that if Mrs. Pellegrino wants to have dinner celebrating your marriage sometime in January, you'd be happy to attend. It will make the future a lot easier on everyone."

We drove back to Poplar House. Marty, Jane, my wife and I had one of their famous waffle breakfasts in a dining room that was completely empty. Then we rode up to our wedding bed and turned off the phone.

We looked out at the park as the first dull glow of the winter sunrise spreading across the park blessed the naked trees of Poplar Grove with the promise of warmth to come.

Speaking of naked, wasn't there something else I should be doing now?

"I could get to like this town," I said. "I think I'll stay here for a while."

My wife drew the blind and opened the top button on the back of her dress. I eased her hand away and continued the task.

40

"You're totally excellent at this sort of thing," my wife said to me much later with considerable complacency. "How did you learn so much about women?"

"I don't know anything about women," I replied. "I know a lot about one woman. I've had the pleasure of studying her for twenty years, and look forward to increasing that pleasure."

"You're so sweet, Petey Pat."

I would frequently have to face that charge.

And God laughed.

My wife and I, hand in hand, walked happily across the park. At the other side, St. Reg's glowed through its stained glass windows like a Chinese lantern. Our chimes rang out "O Holy Night!" Skaters were rapidly fleeing the rink on which we had skated that afternoon on my lady's impulse.

"It's Christmas Eve! We can't spend the whole day in bed!"

The new-fallen snow crunched beneath our feet. The parishioners streaming toward the church walked with a sprightly step and laughed merrily. The magic of Christmas Eve turning to Christmas affected even the most surly and dyspeptic people. By tomorrow at noon, we would all be tired and edgy, but now was the first flourishing of the Christmas spirit.

"Remember our Christmas in second grade, Petey Pat?"

"Nope!"

"You do too! It was the time I sprained my ankle on the skating rink."

"Nor do I remember that I had a hard time helping you off the ice and how you limped back and Fr. Jimmy had to drive you to the hospital and your mother blew up at him—and so did the monsignor."

"That man never had the Christmas spirit . . ."

"Not ever, poor dear man."

"And you lectured the monsignor on the Christmas spirit."

"To no avail."

"They both quieted down. And I came to the midnight Mass on crutches."

"Just don't slip on the ice today."

We were wearing our wedding clothes because we had not thought to bring along anything but jeans and sweatshirts.

We entered the church as the bells began to chime—hurry up, hurry up, hurry up—and the choir went into "The First Noel."

"Quite a wedding feast," I said. "Particularly the dessert."

"Hush," she said with a complacent giggle.

Msgr. Jimmy appeared in the vestibule.

"There are seats at the front of the Gospel side. Your attendants are guarding them."

I glanced around. No sign of either family. We had called my house from Poplar House. I wanted my family to hear about it from us. They were delighted. You'd had to do it that way, Dad said, serves them right. We promised we'd have Christmas dinner with them.

It had not taken the new pastor long to restore the liturgy at St. Reg's. It was tasteful and elegant again. And, somehow, we all sang.

After his homily, he paused, glanced down at us and grinned.

"The shepherds heard the angels sing on the hills with good

news. Christmas is the first hint of the overwhelming good news that only started in Bethlehem and continues to this day of God's overwhelming love for us. We have some special good news here in St. Regis this Christmas. Two young people who were in my First Communion class reunited again here yesterday morning. Peter Kane, known to all of us as Petey Pat, and his longtime unindicted co-conspirator, Mariana Pia Pellegrino, said their vows here this morning. Pete is now Col. Peter Kane of the U.S. Army who has quite literally returned to Poplar Grove from the dead."

The congregation, warmed by the Christmas spirit, applauded! Great story! Hero returns to marry first love!

"Stand up and smile," the first love instructed me.

I did of course, my arm around her mouthwatering waist.

The liturgy continued. Since Jimmy was the vicar for liturgy, it had to be all right.

"Did you see my parents?" she whispered.

"No."

"They're out there! Dad looks like he's ready to go to court."

We encountered our respective families in the vestibule after Mass. They were all very happy. My father and my wife kissed affectionately.

"All's well that ends well," he said. "I'm proud to have you as a daughter-in-law."

"And I'm proud of you, Dad."

Mom hugged her, tears mixing with tears.

Ellen, my lovely sister, rolled her eyes at me and grinned.

If I were to believe the Lord my God, this was all accomplished by a right to the jaw. Only one was enough.

Whatever.

Then my in-laws appeared, Sil breathing fire, Anita taut with rage, ready to explode. She must have won the fight.

"Medal or not, young man, you're out of line on this," Don Silvio said. "Mariana didn't ask our permission."

"I am, as Mom tells me often, an old maid," my wife countered. "The law does not require permission. I thought it better to have this inevitable scene after the ceremony rather than before. You can't stop us, Dad. You never could."

"I will go into court and seek an injunction."

"If you want to make a fool out of yourself, Dad, go ahead."

"You don't have a license to marry."

"Of course we do," I said, drawing the document out of my jacket pocket with the kind of éclat that John Wayne would have displayed in a similar blue uniform. "It's all perfectly legal. I'm disappointed, sir, that you'd think your daughter is such an incompetent lawyer as to forget this."

Msgr. Jimmy, who had drifted up to our little huddle in the corner of the vestibule, shook his head. I was making things worse.

"Monsignor," Sil roared, "I'll have you before the Roman Rota for performing a marriage without announcing the bans as required by Canon Law!"

Jimmy removed a document from the cuff of his monsignorial cassock.

"Here is the dispensation from the bans, signed by our Cardinal Archbishop."

"On what grounds?"

"Let me see, what does it say here? Oh, yes 'unreasonable parental opposition . . .' Besides, Sil, as you well know, failure to announce bans does not invalidate the exchange of consent."

"You have broken my heart, you ungrateful little wretch," Anita sobbed, on the edge of hysteria. "Ever since you were a baby I have planned a wedding for you that would have been just like mine. It has been the dream of my life. Now you have spoiled it. I will never forgive you!"

"One thing you forgot, Mrs. Pellegrino," I said firmly. "It was not your wedding. It was Mariana's."

Sil finally realized what was happening.

"Pete is right, Anita. Mariana was never given a chance to plan her own wedding. She was entitled to a choice."

"It is clear, Silvio, that she has no taste—including in her choice of a groom."

I intervened with the lines Jimmy had taught me in my most charming Irish mode. "If Mr. and Mrs. Pellegrino want to have a dinner celebrating our marriage sometime in January, we'd be happy to attend. That way we can begin this new family on a happy note."

"Everything is open," my wife said, "except the groom and my wedding dress."

She removed her fur coat and gave it to me.

Both her parents gasped, as well they might.

"That is a very generous offer, Pete," Mr. Pellegrino said, shaking hands with me. "Would you give us a ring sometime next week so we can discuss this matter further?"

Quite unaccountably my mother-in-law embraced me.

"Thank you, Peter, thank you! Isn't she beautiful in that wedding dress?"

"Come to think of it, Mom, she really is."

I was back in second grade in the St. Regis school yard. I could cope with my in-laws. No problem.

I was the only one not crying. Well, Msgr. Jimmy wasn't either. With a big grin, he had swept back into the Church.

My wife was still crying when we walked back to our bower. Then she began to laugh.

"You wonderful, shanty Irish faker," she whispered.

"I never had a chance to charm her before."

42

Two lovers on a quiet beach somewhere, hiding under a big umbrella, an empty bottle of red wine between them. The young woman is mostly asleep. The young man reflects.

In second grade I could sense everything she felt, new kid left out. But gorgeous. Too gorgeous. Same thing now. I sense her every mood change, insecurity, desire. I respond without a word; a touch or a hug is enough. She tells me I'm "sweet." Now she adds "sensitive." She does not object to emotional nakedness. More delightful by far than physical nakedness—though that is spectacular too. I should always be reverent.

"Pete, did God send you back from heaven to take care of me?"

"Yes."

"That was very sweet, wasn't it?"

"Sensitive too!"

And God laughed again.

—TUCSON, ARIZONA
ST. VALENTINE'S DAY
2008

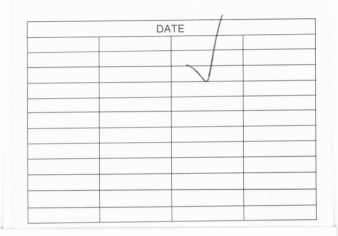